A Murderous Business

ALSO BY CATHY PEGAU

Blood Remains

The Demon Equilibrium

Rulebreaker

Caught in Amber

Deep Deception

Murder on the Last Frontier

Borrowing Death

Murder on Location

A Murderous Business

A HARRIMAN & MANCINI MYSTERY

CATHY PEGAU

MINOTAUR BOOKS
NEW YORK

This is a work of fiction. All of the characters, organizations, and events portrayed in this novel are either products of the author's imagination or are used fictitiously.

First published in the United States by Minotaur Books, an imprint of St. Martin's Publishing Group

EU Representative: Macmillan Publishers Ireland Ltd, 1st Floor, The Liffey Trust Centre, 117–126 Sheriff Street Upper, Dublin 1, D01 YC43

A MURDEROUS BUSINESS. Copyright © 2025 by Cathy Pegau. All rights reserved. Printed in the United States of America. For information, address St. Martin's Publishing Group, 120 Broadway, New York, NY 10271.

www.minotaurbooks.com

Designed by Omar Chapa

The Library of Congress Cataloging-in-Publication Data is available upon request.

ISBN 978-1-250-35648-2 (hardcover)
ISBN 978-1-250-35649-9 (ebook)

The publisher of this book does not authorize the use or reproduction of any part of this book in any manner for the purpose of training artificial intelligence technologies or systems. The publisher of this book expressly reserves this book from the Text and Data Mining exception in accordance with Article 4(3) of the European Union Digital Single Market Directive 2019/790.

Our books may be purchased in bulk for specialty retail/wholesale, literacy, corporate/premium, educational, and subscription box use. Please contact MacmillanSpecialMarkets@macmillan.com.

First Edition: 2025

10 9 8 7 6 5 4 3 2 1

With regards to the important work of Dr. Harvey Wiley and the innovative spirit of Marjorie Merriweather Post, may your legacies continue to inspire.

This book is for the ever-resilient LGBTQIA+ community of the past, present, and future. We have always been here and will always be here.

ONE

The vast grounds of the B&H Foods cannery were too quiet, lifeless but for the birds calling in the April evening. Margot Baxter Harriman hurried up to the double doors of the main building, keys clutched in her hand. Though unlocking the door was an action she'd performed many times, both as a child "helping" her father and in her more recent role as company president, something now made her uneasy.

Don't be silly.

Shaking off the feeling, Margot opened one of the doors that led into the small reception area and paused, soaking in the birdsong, the breeze rustling through the trees, the distant bellow of a steamer on Little Neck Bay. Spring had come to most of New York and the mid-Atlantic states, and with spring came the start of the harvest. Within a few weeks, the cannery would be going all day, most every day, through October. Everything as it should be.

"I'll be right back," she called over her shoulder to her driver.

Bascom nodded to her from the driver's seat of her new burgundy 1912 Cadillac Model Thirty. It may have been Margot's automobile on paper, but it was definitely John Bascom's baby. He "allowed" her to drive only under the narrowest conditions since her first sporadic and somewhat hair-raising lessons in her father's Ford almost a decade ago.

Margot crossed the dimly lit reception area, light coming in from three north-facing windows, her heels marking sure, regular beats across the polished tile floor.

Through a second set of double doors, she passed the time clock and the locker rooms where employees left their coats and other personal items. A final set of doors opened into the main canning facility. With the overhead lights off and only a few small lamps burning, the vast room contained deep pockets of shadows among islands of equipment. Hazy sunlight through rows of high windows marked bulky machinery and long chopping tables.

The absence of sound was alien. Quiet usually didn't bother her, but this room wasn't meant to be silent.

In her head, she heard the chug of motors driving belts

that delivered cans to packers, then to lidders, then to boilers. She heard the rattle of carts of empty cans, the voices of workers, the chop of knives through carrots and potatoes. The sights, sounds, aromas, and flavors of B&H were ingrained in her very being.

Margot hurried across the canning room, to the stairs that led to the windowed observation hall and the upper offices. The ever-present tang of vegetation and metal scented the air, despite the cannery having been closed for three days. Chilled air sent a shiver through her.

As she ascended, she trailed her fingertips along the blue and gold company logo painted on the wall. Her legacy. Her grandparents on both sides had been partners in a produce market, then her parents had taken over, expanding B&H to a cannery, adding a commercial bakery and a distributor. With the death of her father last fall, it was up to Margot to carry on, despite what everyone might think of a woman running a business.

Passing the closed doors of the offices labeled HIRAM POTTER, MANAGER and MARCUS JAMES, DISTRIBUTION, Margot fished her keys from her coat pocket and headed to JULIA BLUMFELD, ACCOUNTANT. Prior to leaving for Montauk for the long holiday weekend, she had asked Julia to gather information for an early Monday presentation to the shareholders. The extremely competent Julia had likely completed the task before Margot set foot on the eastbound train.

She slid the appropriate key into the lock and was met with resistance when she tried to turn it. The door was already unlocked.

Margot hesitated. Had Julia forgotten to lock her office? That would have been completely out of character for the attentive accountant. She knew Margot had her own keys, so there was no need to leave the door unlocked for her. Perhaps security had checked the office and forgotten to lock up behind them? Also unusual. What would have prompted the security guard to be in this office at all? Had there been trouble? A break-in? She should have been contacted.

There had been grumblings from men of business with her transition from "boss's daughter and tolerated vice president" to taking over B&H six months ago; everything needed to run smoothly, to be on the up-and-up. She knew the shareholders would be more than happy to see her fail and try to replace her with someone more "capable." In other words, a man of their ilk. She couldn't let her family legacy slip through her fingers.

Margot pocketed her keys and opened the door. Light from the hall spilled in as she reached for the switch on the wall. She took two steps before she registered what she saw.

Giana Gilroy, retired assistant to Margot's late father, sat at Julia's desk.

"Mrs. Gilroy, what—" The rest of the question lodged in Margot's throat.

Mrs. Gilroy stared at her through half-closed eyes, as if she were on the verge of sleep. One arm rested in her lap, the other on the desk, pen in hand. Her head leaned against the back of Julia's chair, set at a questioning tilt to the left.

What a strange place to take a nap, Margot thought, drowning out the part of her brain that knew what was truly in front of her.

"M-Mrs. Gilroy?" Slowly, Margot walked toward her. She reached out to touch the older woman's shoulder, but hesitated. All too vivid memories of finding her father in a similar position ran through her head.

Margot's racing heart and flipping stomach lurched in opposite directions. She took a step back. Her gaze swept the desktop, searching for something to explain what had happened. The candlestick telephone with the receiver askew on its holder. A desk set with the pen missing. The report Julia had left for her.

And under Mrs. Gilroy's hand, a note addressed to Margot.

TWO

Margot sat in the visitor's chair in Hiram Potter's outer office, a glass of water clutched in both hands as she listened to the police lieutenant and the coroner down the hall. She could hear the tenor of their voices, but not what they were saying, which was both frustrating and a blessing.

Lieutenant Presley strode in, followed by Hiram, who understandably looked rather pale. Margot appreciated Hiram's comforting presence. He'd been her father's best friend and was her godfather; she'd known him her entire life. Despite being called away from his Sunday dinner, Hiram was as smartly dressed in a charcoal pin-striped suit as if this was a regular workday event.

God forbid.

The lieutenant, a man of about Margot's age, wore a crisp brown suit that seemed a touch loose on him. New suit or new position? His blond hair was slicked back, darkened with some sort of oil, and his stiff shirt collar dug into his neck.

"Are you up for some questions, Miss Harriman?" he asked.

This was her company. She had found the body. Did she have a choice?

Before she could respond, Hiram cleared his throat. He'd taken his handkerchief out and dabbed his forehead before folding it neatly, returning it to his trouser pocket.

"Is that really necessary?" He stood beside Margot, a reassuring hand on her shoulder. "Miss Harriman has had quite the upset, Lieutenant. Can't it wait?"

Agitation bristled through Margot, but she smoothed it over with the thought that Hiram was only being protective. He was trying to make the situation less traumatic for her. He'd done so throughout her life, offering solace over some hurt when she was a child, and when her parents had each passed. And yet, the assumption that she was too distraught to answer important questions, that he could speak for her as if she were incapable, reminded her that Hiram wasn't always as keen on her being the president of B&H, or in charge of her own life, as he professed.

"It's fine, Hiram." She sipped the now tepid water, then set the glass on the desk. "Please, Lieutenant, go ahead."

Hiram pursed his lips as he sat in his secretary's chair on the other side of the desk. He wouldn't contradict Margot in front of anyone, though she might hear his thoughts on the matter in private. She wondered if he'd ever truly stop seeing her as Randolph Harriman's little girl—she'd be thirty-three in a few months, for goodness' sake—and instead as the majority owner and operator of B&H, a proper businesswoman in her own right.

Presley retrieved a notebook and pencil from his inner jacket pocket. "What time did you arrive here?"

"About six. The train from Montauk was late. My driver, Bascom, can confirm the time."

"Why didn't you go home?"

"I was picking up a report Julia Blumfeld left for me. I have an early meeting tomorrow in the city."

Presley scratched the information into his book. "The papers on her desk?"

Margot shifted slightly on the chair. "That's right."

"You came in on the train from Montauk. What were you doing out there?"

"Visiting friends for the weekend. The Keatings." Why was this about her?

"When did you leave town?"

Margot quirked an eyebrow at him. Was he establishing

general whereabouts or asking something else? The lieutenant stared back at her, pencil poised.

"Thursday, on the noon train."

"Why didn't you drive?"

"Everyone had the weekend off, including my driver and other house staff. After the Thursday shift ended, the cannery closed as well."

"About seven that evening," Hiram added. "I was the last one out and locked up."

Presley narrowed his gaze at her. "Company *and* house staff were off this weekend?"

"For the most part," she said. "The second weekend in April is a company holiday. My parents started it ages ago to celebrate my mother's birthday. That, and the harvest hasn't gotten into full swing yet, so closing doesn't hurt. No one but security guards are on the grounds, usually."

"No one else around all weekend?" The lieutenant seemed incredulous. "Who knew that was going to be the situation?"

Margot and Hiram exchanged looks. The April holiday had so long been part of the B&H routine that they hardly thought about it.

"Everyone," Margot said. "It was no secret."

Presley frowned as if he disapproved of such frivolity. "Only security on the grounds. Mrs. Gilroy would have known this?"

"Of course," she said.

"When was the last time you saw her?"

Margot swallowed down the lump that suddenly formed in her throat. She took a sip of water. "October. My father's funeral."

Nearly six months. Could that be right?

"She had retired in September," Hiram said.

"And she lived nearby? Did she have family? A husband?"

"No, she was widowed, and they had no children. She lived somewhere in Long Island City." Hiram gestured toward his inner office. "I have the address and family contact, if you want it."

Presley did. Hiram rose, straightening his tie while looking at Margot. She nodded once, resisting the urge to roll her eyes. She would be fine without him sitting there for the two minutes it would take him to retrieve the information.

"Why do you suppose she came here?" the lieutenant asked. He ran his pinky between his snug collar and the flushed skin of his neck.

Margot shook her head, wondering the same. "I have no idea. Mrs. Gilroy was very dear to my father, to my family."

Yet she hadn't seen the woman for months, nor written more than a dashed-off note last month to accompany a silk scarf sent for her birthday. The folded note in Margot's pocket seemed to grow ten times its size, surely alerting the lieutenant of its presence.

Dearest Margot,
I wish there was an easier way to tell you what I need to say. Perhaps you will think me a coward for choosing a note rather than speaking to you in person . . .

Her stomach clenched, thinking of the rest. She couldn't let anyone read it. Not until she understood what it meant. Maybe not ever.

Why had Mrs. Gilroy chosen to come to the cannery if she needed to contact Margot? She couldn't have known Margot would be stopping by. Mrs. Gilroy meant to have the note found, if not by Margot or the house staff, then by Julia Blumfeld. Why?

"How do you suppose she got here?" Presley asked with a raised brow. "Walked or cab from the train station?"

Margot blinked at him, thinking for a moment. "Either, I suppose. A number of our employees come to work on the train or streetcar if they don't live close enough to walk."

"There was a set of keys found in her coat pocket."

"She had keys when she worked here, of course. I thought she'd turned them in when she retired." Though apparently not.

Presley grunted and flipped back through a few pages of his notebook. "No sign of forced entry or any other damage in or around the building." He met her gaze again. "And you noticed nothing unusual when you came in?"

Only the quiet. But that wasn't what he was asking.

She shook her head. "No, but I wasn't looking for anything either. Nothing stood out."

Hiram returned with a sheet of paper that he handed to the lieutenant. "Her address and next of kin. Mrs. Letitia Jacobs. A cousin, I believe."

"Did you notice anything strange about Mrs. Gilroy last time you saw her, Mr. Potter?" Presley asked.

Hiram thought for a moment. "Nothing. Last time I saw her was at Randolph's funeral as well. We were all bereft and not ourselves, of course."

"Of course." Presley jotted. "No idea what would have brought her here?"

"Not an inkling."

The lieutenant started to ask another question when the coroner walked in. He was a man of middle years, hair mostly gray, and somberly dressed, as befitting his position. He checked his gold watch and addressed Presley as he slipped it back into his vest pocket.

"Heart failure, I'd say on first looks, Lieutenant, but I'll have more after the postmortem tomorrow."

"Natural causes?" Presley wrote in his book.

"So it seems."

"That doesn't answer the question of why she was here," Margot said.

Though they'd been introduced, the medical man looked at her as if seeing her for the first time. "That isn't my concern, miss."

He turned his attention back to the lieutenant before he even finished the sentence, dismissing her out of hand.

Margot stared at him with bemusement bordering on irritation. "Miss," as if she were some random person who had wandered into B&H. Had he not bothered to remember this was *her* building?

The coroner turned to leave the room.

"My men are going to take her down now. I suggest those with delicate senses"—he glanced at Margot—"remain where they are for the time being."

Delicate senses?

Margot was caught between bristling and laughing. It wasn't the first time others—particularly men—had assumed she was demure and squeamish. Though to be fair, she had no desire to leave her chair while the coroner's men performed their task.

"Well, seems we have everything wrapped up," Presley said, shutting his book.

Margot blinked. "But how she was just sitting there—"

She was interrupted by clatter and voices out in the hall. Someone laughed, and she cringed. It felt terribly out of place.

"You heard the coroner. Natural causes." The lieutenant shrugged. "If you can come up with a reason why Mrs. Gilroy would come here, feel free to let me know. In the meantime, I believe I have all I need. Good evening."

He tipped his hat and left the office.

The letter in Margot's pocket grew heavier.

Three

The clock on the mantel struck ten thirty. Margot sat at the massive desk that had been her father's, the note from Mrs. Gilroy on the blotter before her. She held a weighty cut glass tumbler of Dewar's in one hand.

She should have been getting ready for bed. The shareholders' meeting the next morning would require her to be alert and attentive. She could have contacted them to cancel or reschedule, considering the circumstances, but she wouldn't risk it. The moment those men in their smart suits and with rosewater in their hair sensed she was anything less than one hundred percent—hell, two hundred percent—they would press for her resignation.

And if any got wind of what was written in Mrs. Gilroy's neat script? Margot shuddered at the thought and took in a slow, calming breath.

The aromas of leather and dust and old pipe tobacco lingered in the paneled office. The scents reminded her of her father, kept him close to her, like her mother's perfumes upstairs. Smells that brought back loving memories. Margot smiled as she recalled sitting on her parents' bed as her mother, Camille, dressed for a business dinner. While dabbing on a touch of her signature violet scent, she'd explained how important it was to be confident before those who would challenge women in business.

Margot remembered standing at this very desk, at her father's side, as he expounded on plans for B&H. He'd spoken to her like he'd expected Margot to take his place since her first breath. Still, he'd never let her assume her position was a given; she'd had to earn it.

Margot sipped her drink, the alcohol soothing her nerves as it burned her sinuses. There was no need to open the note again. The words were imprinted on her brain in stark black.

Dearest Margot,
I wish there was an easier way to tell you what I
need to say. Perhaps you will think me a coward for
choosing a note rather than speaking to you in person.
I can't argue that.

Best to get right to it, I suppose.

Your father and I were involved in a situation at B&H. People got sick. Some died. There is no way we can be accountable for those actions now, but I fear the practice continues at B&H as well as other companies. You can stop it.

Let

It ended there with a stray squiggle of ink trailing off the bottom of the *t*. No closing. No signature. But she recognized Mrs. Gilroy's precise handwriting, shaky as it was.

Mrs. Gilroy had obviously meant to say more, but what? What had been so dreadful, so stressful, that her heart had given out then and there?

Margot might never know.

But what she'd read disturbed her to the core. *People got sick. Some died.* What was going on at B&H?

Of course she was aware that some producers used questionable practices to make their foods more shelf-stable, or added fillers to stretch contents while claiming their products were "pure." It was still happening today, though not in nearly the frequency prior to the 1906 federal law. Doctor Harvey Wiley had been pointing out such atrocities and calling for safer foods and medicines for years. His bulletins had been regular reading in the Harriman household throughout her childhood and into her early years at Mount Holyoke.

Her parents had made sure B&H products were honest well before the federal law was enacted. There were companies that only said as much; B&H had meant it. Canneries and plants were regularly inspected for procedure and cleanliness. Margot pored over the inspectors' reports after each visit to every B&H site. Never had she observed or read anything untoward.

Your father and I were involved in a situation at B&H.

Had Margo seen everything in those reports? Or had she been shown only what she needed to see? What they had wanted her to see?

Her stomach churned at the very idea that Randolph had compromised B&H, putting people at risk. That was not the man she knew. Or he hadn't been.

She had returned to the house after the interview with Lieutenant Presley and gone through every drawer and file in the home office. Nothing. Not a hint of misdeeds. Not that she knew what, exactly, she was looking for.

Margot drained the last finger of whisky in a single gulp. Anger and confusion warred within her, churning the alcohol in her gut and sparking the throb of a headache. What was going on? How could her father have condoned anything that might threaten B&H?

She'd had to prove herself to Randolph—to Hiram, to the shareholders, to everyone—time and time again. But if he had been doing something untoward while she strived to uphold the standards *he* had set?

Margot's hand tightened around the cut glass tumbler.

"Miss Harriman?"

Margot looked up. Bascom stood in the doorway, tie still snug against his collar and silvering hair still neatly combed, despite the late hour. She couldn't recall ever seeing him disheveled. She forced her body to relax, hoping nothing showed on her face. She had taught herself to maintain a mask no matter what thoughts were forming underneath. Her mother's words as she herself had navigated the trappings of being a woman in business and society echoed in Margot's head: *Don't let them see you flinch.*

"Yes?"

Bascom glanced around the office, his gaze lingering on the empty glass on the desk, likely noting the low level of whisky in the decanter within Margot's reach. "When would you like to depart tomorrow morning?"

She grinned at his subtle hint that it was time for bed. "By seven. Seven thirty at the latest. I've asked Caroline to have breakfast ready around six fifteen."

It would take them nearly three quarters of an hour to drive into Manhattan. Margot preferred to be at the hotel early, to watch the others arrive. She'd sit in a quiet corner until they all entered the meeting room before joining them. It was a petty, "You will wait for me, not the other way around," maneuver she'd learned from her father, but it also gave her the opportunity to see what sort of mood the men were in. Handling everyone from shareholders to customers to employees required understanding them and their concerns.

Bascom nodded once. "Very good. I'll see you in the morning. Good night."

He turned to leave, but Margot called him back. "John, wait a moment."

Bascom faced her once again, head slightly tilted. She rarely used his given name. "Miss?"

Margot gestured for him to come into the office. He obliged, closing the heavy door behind him, and stood before the desk, hands clasped behind his back.

"Have you any sort of ear to the ground at the cannery or the other facilities? Heard about anything going on?"

It was a risk to ask him, though B&H doings were probably not something in which he'd be involved. Bascom was considered a "house" employee rather than a company employee. But who could she question at B&H without tipping her hand? Hiram seemed to be the best candidate, but if her father had been doing something he shouldn't have, Hiram would have been part of it, or at the very least known about it. Wouldn't he?

Confusion flickered across Bascom's face. "Nothing I'm aware of. Do you have a specific activity in mind?"

"I'd rather not go into it." Margot gently rolled the tumbler between her hands. "I need you to find someone for me, John."

"Anyone in particular?"

"Someone to look into . . . events and circumstances. Someone discreet." She moistened her dry lips before continuing, looking him straight in the eye. "Someone not averse to bending rules, if necessary."

He was quiet for a moment. "I believe there are a few such individuals I can contact, Miss Harriman."

Margot settled back against the leather chair. "Thank you, John."

"Of course, miss. I'll see you in the morning."

She bade him good night and poured another finger of whisky after the door closed softly behind him.

Four

Margot stood in front of a five-story brick building on West 57th Street. Drivers navigated their horses or horsepower down the road while pedestrians dashed here and there. Motorcar and carriage wheels crunched grit, hooves clomped past. The stink of garbage, equine, and exhaust wasn't as terrible as some streets, but it was no rose garden either. On the corner, a newsboy hawked his papers with the latest headlines about the recent *Titanic* disaster.

Margot shuddered. *Those poor souls.*

What happened in the frigid Atlantic was beyond terrible, but out of her power. Events at B&H were not. She had to focus on what, with any luck, she could fix.

She glanced down at the square of paper in her hand, comparing the address written in Bascom's neat print to that on the plaque beside the blue arched door. There was no indication of went on within.

"Well, you asked for discreet," she muttered to herself.

Discreet and out of the purview of those who would jump at the chance to find fault with her.

The shareholders' meeting two days before had gone well enough, though Margot had forced herself not to think of Mrs. Gilroy and the note. The dozen stodgy men sitting around the long oak table had peppered her with questions regarding B&H's current financial status, projected profits, and future endeavors. Those were their main concerns, of course, and they responded to her answers with reluctant grunts of approval. Thank goodness for Julia Blumfeld's stellar report and her own understanding of the business. Something she had to prove all too frequently.

Not until the very end of the meeting did one of them remark about the "incident." Several had known Mrs. Gilroy and her connection to the Harriman family and expressed their condolences. There was a brief discussion of how Mrs. Gilroy being found at B&H would reflect on the company, but Margot assured them that, as unusual as the circumstances seemed, there was no indication anyone at B&H was at fault.

At least, not for Mrs. Gilroy's death.

What Mrs. Gilroy alluded to in her note was another

matter altogether. If there was something illicit going on, Margot would be held accountable. If people were hurt or dead, there'd be no mercy. The papers would lambaste her and B&H. If the company survived, the stockholders would find a way to force her out. She'd lose everything.

Thankfully, as promised, Bascom had found her the address of someone who might be able to help.

He'd been reluctant to let her go unaccompanied, but Margot had assured him she could manage. Besides, a Cadillac waiting at the curb would draw too much attention.

The single glass and wood door at the top of the stairs was unlocked. Margot pulled it open and entered the lobby. To her left, a list of vague company names that occupied the first three floors. They could have been anything from accounting firms to piano tuners. There was nothing listed for the upper two floors. Were they apartments? Storage? Or did the occupants prefer not to be so public?

You're being overdramatic.

The office she wanted was on the third floor.

There was no sign of an elevator, so Margot started up the stairs, lifting the hem of her day dress to keep from tripping. The halls were quiet as she passed the first two floors, dust motes floating in the dim light coming from ceiling fixtures. On the third floor, she found number 307 with MANCINI & ASSOCIATES painted in black on the frosted glass of the door. She hesitated. Was she supposed to knock or go in?

She settled on both, knocking as she turned the brass knob and pushed the door open. The outer office of Mancini & Associates contained a wooden desk, several filing cabinets, a few pictures on the walls, and an attractive, buxom brunette with a honey-brown complexion wearing wire-rimmed spectacles. She held a telephone earpiece to her head as she jotted on a sheet of paper with her left hand.

"Uh-huh," the woman said into the mouthpiece as she smiled and waved Margot in. She gestured toward a ladder-back chair with a green upholstered seat. "Yeah, yeah, okay. You sure?"

Her accent had hints of the Lower East Side.

Margot sat down, hands folded in her lap. She glanced around the outer office while she tried to avoid eavesdropping. Or at least appear that she wasn't eavesdropping. The conversation she heard wasn't particularly interesting or revealing, and after a few more "Right," "Got it," and other short responses, there was a final "Thanks," before the earpiece was set in the holder.

The woman, who appeared to be about ten years younger than Margot, removed her glasses and rose from her chair, hand out. Her crisp white shirtwaist and green-and-gold tartan skirt were simple but well-made. "Good morning. I'm Loretta Mancini."

Margot stood to shake her hand. It was a good handshake, firm and reassuring. There was an energy about this woman;

she was confident, but relaxed. In charge. Miss Mancini's brown eyes showed interest and intelligence, with long black lashes under thick, well-shaped eyebrows.

"Margot Harriman. How do you do, Miss Mancini?" They released each other's hands, and Margot returned to her seat at Miss Mancini's gesture.

"Can I get you some tea or coffee?"

"Coffee, if you please."

Margot watched Miss Mancini as she poured coffee from a pot wrapped in a cozy into two china cups painted with a delicate vine motif.

"Cream and sugar?" she asked.

"Both, if you please. One lump."

Miss Mancini fixed her coffee and placed two shortbread cookies from a package near the coffeepot onto the saucer. The package had the familiar silhouette of "Auntie Em" beside the B&H logo.

Margot accepted the refreshments and picked up a cookie. "My favorite," she said with a grin.

Bascom may have confided in Mancini & Associates that she was the one arriving. Had Miss Mancini chosen the cookies with Margot in mind?

"Mine too," the other woman said, returning to her chair behind the desk. "But the coffee is Castor's. It's smoother yet more robust, in my opinion."

Margot swallowed a mouthful of her competitor's brew; she wasn't wrong. "I'll have to speak to our coffee division."

Miss Mancini let out a bark of a laugh, and Margot immediately decided she liked the younger woman.

"Are you the Mancini or the associates in Mancini and Associates?"

"Both, I suppose," Miss Mancini replied. "My father retired from the police department and opened this office not long after. My brother went into the seminary, and my sister married an electrician. I started working here well before it was probably proper."

Margot gave a small, understanding smile. "I know how that goes."

Miss Mancini shared an enigmatic smile in return. "Indeed."

She set some papers aside and put a clean piece in front of her on the blotter. Pen in her left hand, she sipped her coffee using the other. "Would you care to give me some preliminary information regarding your needs, Miss Harriman?"

Margot glanced at the door marked PRIVATE. "Is Mr. Mancini not in?"

Miss Mancini shifted on her seat. "He isn't, but he should be here shortly. I usually take down initial information from clients and make notes during meetings." She must have seen the uncertainty in Margot's face, for she quickly added, "I assure you, discretion and privacy are as important to us as they are to you. When Albert is speaking with a client, he's concentrating on the conversation and asking questions. I ensure information is accurate when he reexamines case notes. Nothing goes beyond these walls. But if you'd rather I didn't attend or take notes, that's your prerogative, of course." She leveled her gaze at Margot. "I'm not unused to such situations."

A challenge, from one businesswoman to another? Acknowledgment of their gendered predicament? Margot had never been denied access to meetings, but she knew what it was like to be underestimated yet fully capable.

"I'm sure I can place my faith in your procedure," she said.

Unless you prove otherwise, was the unspoken implication. Regardless of the situation, as in most business arrangements, the word and trust of each party meant as much as the hoped-for success. Reputation was crucial. A few unkind words by someone in Margot's social circle could possibly affect an outfit like Mancini & Associates.

Miss Mancini nodded, a solemn expression on her face. "Thank you, Miss Harriman. We'll endeavor to maintain that faith. Now, how can we help?"

Margot noticed that the Lower East Side accent was no longer present, and hadn't been since Miss Mancini hung up the telephone. Quite the chameleon, this young woman, to adjust to her clientele.

What Margot had to reveal wasn't the easiest thing to discuss with a perfect stranger—the suspicion that her father, her company, had been or could still be doing something dangerous or illegal. The B&H reputation for providing good food was paramount, to be protected at all costs. If any of what she was about to tell Miss Mancini was true, if even the idea of the possibility was made public, B&H was done. *She* was done. She'd be dragged through the papers as "proof" that having a "naïve woman" in charge was problematic. But she couldn't allow whatever might be happening to continue, either.

"Miss Harriman?"

Margot looked up at the woman, aware she hadn't responded, and gave her a wan smile. "My apologies, Miss Mancini. This is a very difficult and delicate topic. I can't have any of it become public knowledge, whether it turns out to be what I fear or not. Even a rumor of such events could devastate my company."

Understanding softened Miss Mancini's intense gaze. "Which is why you're here and not going to the police with whatever troubles you."

It wasn't a question. She must have known precautions and discretion were required. That's what her clients came here for, after all.

Margot felt some tension melt from her shoulders. "Yes, exactly."

"While we have to look to others for information at times,

we make every effort to maintain absolute privacy and restrict what we share only as necessary to get results." Miss Mancini folded her hands on top of the desk. "We'll discuss beforehand what you feel comfortable using to that end and will never go beyond those limits."

"Of course," Margot said with a grin. "I understand certain paths might need to be taken."

Miss Mancini smiled sweetly and set her pen aside. A gesture meant to put Margot at ease, to make this more of a conversation than an interview? "Why don't you tell me what's going on?"

Margot took a slow, deep breath. "This past Sunday, I stopped by the cannery to pick up a report." She proceeded to tell the other woman about finding Mrs. Gilroy dead at the accountant's desk. She opened her purse, removed the folded, cream-colored paper that had weighed on her mind for the last several days, and handed it over. "Near her was this."

Miss Mancini took the note and unfolded it. She frowned as she reached the end. "What is she talking about?"

"I don't know, exactly."

The younger woman looked up. A single dark eyebrow rose. "Not exactly? What do you *think* she means?"

There would be no going back if she spoke now, but what choice did she have?

"Despite knowing better, as well as disregarding regulations and laws, some companies use additives or fillers to make their foods last longer or to dilute the product. Or they cut corners in other ways. Many of these are not particularly good for people."

"Or can even be deadly as chemicals accumulate in the body," Miss Mancini said. She shrugged at Margot's obvious surprise at her knowledge. "I read about Doctor Wiley's Poison Squad in the papers. I've always had a keen interest in gathering information of all sorts."

The famous—infamous, to some in the foods industry—chemist and his research that led to the 1906 Pure Food and Drug Act were all over the newspapers across the country. The studies had caused quite the ruckus, pointing out terrible practices that eventually required food producers to take better steps toward consumer health and well-being. The recently ratified Sherley Amendment would provide similar provisions for labeling medicines. Newspapers had been reporting on the amendment for months, bringing up cases of unexplained illnesses that could potentially be attributed to the foods or drugs patients ingested.

Margot was aware some companies still skirted the laws. She just hadn't expected the possibility of one of them being her own.

Miss Mancini held the note up. "Your Mrs. Gilroy was writing a final confession about such activities within B&H. That she and your father were involved in something that cost lives."

Another nonquestion.

Having someone else say aloud the very thing Margot was most afraid of hit like a punch in the gut. She closed her eyes for a moment and swallowed hard. Looking at Miss Mancini again, she steadied the quiver in her chest. *Don't let them see you flinch.* "Yes. But I've never been witness to anything at B&H, nor have I found anything in my father's papers so far to suggest it."

"All you have is this note and—"

"Concerns," Margot finished for her. "The newspapers are on alert for the slightest whiff of wrongdoing. Even if what's in the note is not true, the rumor itself could cause damage. I need to know what, if anything, is going on, and I can't see a way of looking into things myself without raising questions or risking word getting out."

Miss Mancini nodded, a thoughtful expression on her face. "A quiet investigation. No attachment to you or your circle." Her gaze became intense as she focused on Margot. "Can you get someone in as an employee without raising suspicion of a connection to you?"

"It's nearly time for the early harvest," Margot said. "We'll be increasing production and taking on seasonal workers, so yes, that should be easy enough."

The other woman grinned. "Excellent."

Margot shifted uncomfortably. Miss Mancini had mentioned using other resources but she hadn't expected the possibility so soon. "Who would you have go into the cannery?"

She didn't want any more people than necessary with knowledge of the situation.

"Why, me of course," Miss Mancini said, as if it was the most natural idea in the world.

Five

Rett watched Margot Baxter Harriman arch one perfectly shaped eyebrow, putting an entire query into that singular gesture: Who did Loretta Mancini think she was?

Rett knew the answer to that, at least. She was the daughter of Albert and Rosa Mancini, a second-generation American woman determined to make her way, on her own terms. With or without her parents' support.

"I'm not just a secretary or receptionist." Rett sat up straighter, her gaze never leaving the woman before her. "I've assisted with cases in the past."

Granted, most of that was simple observation, or questions to desk sergeants or friends and family of whoever might be involved in a case. But she was ready for more, even if Albert didn't realize it.

"Have you ever operated secretly, as you suggest?" Miss Harriman was expressionless. Even in their short time together, Rett had noticed she rarely let any sort of emotion cross her face.

Rett considered exaggerating her experience, but fibbing was no way to start off a business relationship. Or any relationship, truth be told. She'd learned that lesson the hard way.

"Here and there. I've made inquiries without revealing who I was or what I was after, as is the nature of our business." She rose from her chair and went around to the front of the desk. "I know what I'm doing, Miss Harriman. Just give me a chance. You don't have to pay me if I don't get results."

Free anything usually got people to agree, even those who could afford to pay. Maybe especially those who could afford it. Rich folks tended to be tight with their purse strings.

"What about Mr. Mancini?" Miss Harriman asked, nodding toward Albert's office door.

What about Albert?

Rett decided honesty was still the best policy with this woman. "Albert has been . . . ill off and on for the last few months, Miss Harriman. He's taken on a case or two, but I'm pretty much running the show. I'll discuss this with him, or you can wait and speak with him directly, but it sounds like you need to move as quickly as possible."

She watched for any indication of Margot Baxter Harriman's thoughts, but, as before, couldn't nail down what was going through the woman's head.

Miss Harriman then crossed her arms and looked down at her lap. Rett was no body language expert, but she could read most people and recognized "How do I let her down?" when she saw it. Damn. There went that opportunity. She needed this job; with Albert doing less elbow rubbing with potential clients, cases had been thinning like a cheap wig.

While Rett prepared her counterpoint, Miss Harriman lifted her head. Something in her face and bearing had changed; her chin was up, and her dark eyes held Rett's. Intense. Intelligent. Determined. It took everything in Rett's power not to look away.

She must be a formidable opponent in the boardroom, Rett mused.

"I have to know what's happening in my company. The truth, no matter who is involved, no matter what it is. But it's absolutely imperative that nothing goes public. Not a word." Hope fluttered in Rett's belly. Miss Harriman's fists tightened around her purse, which perfectly matched the dove-gray pinstripes of her cream-colored ensemble. "Do you think you can do that?"

Rett swallowed the doubt that threatened to steal both her voice and the chance to prove herself. "I do."

Miss Harriman relaxed, her fists loosening and worry

lines smoothing as she rose. She opened her purse, removed several folded bills, and handed them to Rett. "For your time today and expenses you may incur. Let me know if you need more. Come to the house tonight. I'll have Bascom pick you up here at seven, if that's convenient."

"That would be very convenient. Thank you." Rett placed the bills on her desk, surprised at how calm she sounded, considering her heart was racing to beat heck. "I appreciate this opportunity, Miss Harriman."

She held the doorknob, half turned toward Rett. "One of the things I promised myself, Miss Mancini, was that I'd give enterprising young women as much support as I could, when I could. But that doesn't mean I'll expect less from you than I would a man."

"Of course not," Rett said, somewhat incensed. "A job done is a job done right, no matter who carries it out."

"Precisely. I'll see you this evening. Good day, Miss Mancini."

"Good day, Miss Harriman."

After the door closed behind the woman, Rett sat down on the corner of her desk. The smile on her face made her cheeks ache.

She raised her fists in triumph. "Yes!"

Now she just had to keep this from Albert.

Six

Rett stepped out of the Cadillac when Bascom opened the passenger door, looked up at the Harrimans's Bayside mansion, and gave a low whistle. Even the air smelled richer out here, half an hour's ride from Rett's own cold-water walk-up. Money definitely helped escape close living, smokestacks, and trash.

Outdoor sconces and light posts provided sufficient illumination to get an idea of the size of the house. It was huge. And sprawling. Everyone in her building could have lived in it with room to spare. Hell, maybe everyone on her block.

"This way, Miss Mancini," Bascom said.

Rett tore her gaze from the three-story stone and cedar

home. Sure, it was large, but the house actually looked like it was someplace to live in, not just for show.

She followed Bascom up to the cherrywood-stained door. He opened it and let her precede him into the foyer. The entirety of her apartment could fit in the entry hall with room to spare.

"Holy Hannah." Rett gawked like some rube from the boondocks seeing Times Square for the first time.

A staircase and doorway on the right and another doorway on the left were lit by a chandelier suspended from the high ceiling. The polished hardwood floor stretched across the room to a wall of portraits that branched off to hallways.

Bascom knocked as he opened the door on the right, checking the room. "She isn't down yet. Would you care for some sort of refreshment while you wait? Tea? Coffee?"

Rett was half tempted to ask for a beer, just to see if she could get any reaction from the stoic man. Though she guessed he wouldn't so much as blink twice at the request. "Tea would be great. Thanks."

Bascom nodded as she slipped past him, into the paneled office. He partially closed the door behind her. Brisk footsteps receded across the foyer.

The room had a distinctly masculine quality about it. The scent of leather and tobacco surrounded the two walls of bookcases and the heavy, thick-legged couch and chairs. Old aromas embedded in the fabrics and surfaces. This had to have been Randolph Harriman's office, now appropriated by his extremely capable daughter.

There were no papers on the desk to peek at, though two tall, wooden filing cabinets were tucked into a corner. It would be rather rude to rifle through your employer's drawers, as tempting as that might be. She wasn't there to investigate the Harrimans. At least, not yet.

"Sorry to keep you waiting, Miss Mancini."

Rett turned around and took Margot Harriman's offered hand when she came closer. She had changed out of the suit she'd worn to Rett's office and now wore a simple but luxurious blue silk dress. Her thick, chestnut hair was still in its heavy, coiled style from earlier. Rett tried not to be jealous of the woman's wardrobe, especially when Miss Harriman greeted her with a genuine smile. Rett had seen her share of hoity-toity fake smiles upon meeting folks like herself. This was not one of those.

"Not a problem. Figured you're busy. Your home is magnificent."

Miss Harriman glanced around the roomy office, wearing an expression Rett could only call wistful. "It's more house than we need, but my father grew up with the notion of showing prosperity to attract prosperity."

She gestured for Rett to take one of the oxblood leather chairs on the visitor's side of the desk. Rett complied. "You don't follow that notion?"

Miss Harriman headed to one of the corner filing cabinets and opened the top drawer. "Not particularly. Don't get me wrong," she said, sorting through loose papers. "I'm the first to admit I enjoy the trappings of my station." She pulled a two-foot-long cardboard tube from the drawer, slammed it shut, and faced Rett. "My advantages aren't lost on me, Miss Mancini, and I do my best to remember that. But there are times when I'd rather . . . not be part of the pretense."

Tough life. Rett squashed the sardonic thought. Miss Harriman seemed like the real deal. So far.

She strode over to Rett and fished a roll of papers from the tube in her hand. Laying the cardboard holder on the floor, she spread the oversized sheets atop the desk and weighed down the corners with various items at hand—a bronze pen-and-ink set, an empty tumbler, a brass paperweight, and a smooth white rock half the size of Rett's fist.

"The B&H cannery," she said. "Original buildings on this top page. Additions and detailed drawings underneath. If you're going to look around, it would be best to know where you're going."

Rett fished her glasses from her purse, scanned the first drawing, then lifted the subsequent pages. She squinted down at the precise, tiny print detailing the architectural drawings. "You've expanded quite a bit over the years."

"We have," Miss Harriman said, nodding thoughtfully. "Sometimes too quickly."

"What do you mean?" Construction of buildings took time, as did corporate empires. Rome wasn't built in a day, and all that.

Miss Harriman shuffled the sheets aside until she reached the third or fourth one down. "We bought a small metalworks and made it our can and machine shop. With seasons sometimes being fickle, having it on the grounds was convenient. We could have some cans made to cover any gaps in shipments from larger manufacturers. The initial costs, however, were more than what B&H could afford out of pocket at the time." Rett couldn't help showing her surprise. She had thought B&H had been rolling in dough from day one. Miss Harriman noticed her reaction. "Not unusual. Most of the company worth is tied up in nonliquid assets, not sitting in a bank waiting to be used. My father wanted to move fast, so he secured a small loan. Took almost five years to pay it back in full."

Rett didn't think five years was all that long for whatever business folks considered a "small loan," but apparently in the corporate world, it was significant.

"Your family has been quite successful, with minimal low points," she said. "Disputes over employee wages that led to short strikes. Run-ins with unions as well as union busters."

She had done some homework on her new client, most of which came from newspapers. B&H was relatively boring, in the grand scheme of things. They went about their business and did well enough. Same for Margot Baxter Harriman herself.

Other than society page bits and bobs saying she was at some charity function or business gathering, there was little about her to be gleaned. Though her position as president of B&H was met with some less than subtle derision, there had never been anything approaching a scandal.

Miss Harriman offered her a crooked grin. "Nothing devastating, at any rate. In the early years we lived off savings, thanks to my mother's forethought. And again, relative to the average person, we were doing more than fine. But any scent of blood and there could have been marketing or buyout pressures from other companies. Mother and Dad were very careful about who was privy to financial information—before there were shareholders, of course. B&H company bills were paid, and we never had to turn away employees or close down. Knock wood."

She rapped on the desktop three times.

"And nothing more controversial than your father handing the company over to you."

Miss Harriman's smile turned brittle. "The business world and the public will get used to it."

"Indeed." Rett gave her a reassuring nod and changed the subject. "When can you get me started at the cannery?"

"I'll tell the floor manager and the receptionist to expect you on Monday." She gathered up the sheets of drawings and began to roll them. "I'll say you're the daughter of one of my house employees, or of a merchant I frequent. We've often arranged jobs that way, so it won't be unusual."

"I'll be there."

"Since we aren't sure which aspect of B&H Mrs. Gilroy was referring to, we'll start there and move on to other facilities like the bakery later." Miss Harriman slid the sheets into the cardboard tube. "Mrs. Gilroy's funeral is Friday morning. I'll be attending, of course."

"I'd offer to go, but perhaps we shouldn't be seen in the same place," Rett said. And chances were she wouldn't recognize anyone anyway.

The other woman thought about it. "I think you're correct."

"But we should meet after the funeral to see if anyone of note was there or nearby."

She looked . . . pleasantly surprised? Very hard to tell what Margot Baxter Harriman was thinking or feeling. "Excellent idea. I'll come by your office at two o'clock, if that's doable."

Rett made a mental note to have her mother keep Albert busy Friday. One of his random arrivals at the office would cause more trouble than she wanted to deal with under the best of circumstances. Having him drop in while she and Miss Harriman discussed a case he wasn't involved in would be terribly embarrassing, to say the least.

"The Castor coffee will be freshly brewed," she said with a small teasing smile.

Miss Harriman laughed and shook her head. "Let me give you some more background on B&H."

SEVEN

Mrs. Gilroy's funeral at Saint Stephen's parish was a small affair. Margot and Hiram arrived together, sitting several pews behind Mrs. Gilroy's cousin, Mrs. Letitia Jacobs, and her husband, Calvin. Neither of the Jacobses chose to say anything during the service; Margot knew who they were only because Father Tierney acknowledged them. There were another two dozen or so in attendance, but no one Margot recognized.

That didn't mean no one knew anything.

"Giana Gilroy moved into the neighborhood as a young bride and immediately became part of the Saint Stephen's family," the priest said.

Someone sniffed loudly then blew their nose.

It had been necessary for Margot to set her feelings aside after finding Mrs. Gilroy in Julia's office. She had focused on the note, on what could be happening at B&H. But now, sitting among mourners, hearing about the woman she'd never get the chance to know better, it felt like a stone was being pushed through her chest.

"She organized the New Mothers Helpers group that collected items for young families and was one of our dear coffee ladies for years."

Margot struggled to keep her emotions in check as the priest's words about Mrs. Gilroy's life and service to the community created a well of grief she hadn't expected. It was hard to believe she had known the woman for two-thirds of her life. Widowed at a relatively young age, Mrs. Gilroy had applied to be Randolph's secretary twenty years ago. She and Margot's mother, Camille, had worked in tandem to keep Randolph on track.

Mrs. Gilroy became more than her father's secretary. She was his personal assistant. She was a friend. She'd seen Margot and her father through the anguish of losing her mother, then kept Randolph focused until Margot was of age and able to take on more responsibility at B&H once she graduated college. After Camille had passed, Mrs. Gilroy had taken over the role of fostering that growth in Margot. She'd *believed* in Margot.

When Randolph started having his "episodes," Mrs. Gilroy had done her best to keep him calm, allowing Margot to maintain a steady rudder at B&H. Their personal relationship slipped away, though she had never doubted Mrs. Gilroy's dedication to Randolph. She'd *meant* to visit with Mrs. Gilroy, but something always came up.

If she'd been more of a friend, more present, would Mrs. Gilroy and Randolph have ever gotten into this mess?

She couldn't say. And it was too late to fix something she should have noticed was broken long ago.

Margot sniffed indelicately. Hiram passed her a crisp, folded white handkerchief; not the one he tended to take out to fold and refold during the day. She accepted it with a quiet thanks and dabbed her eyes and runny nose. Ladies' handkerchiefs weren't sturdy enough for multiple nose blowings, as if women couldn't produce any moisture, even when sad.

When Father Tierney finished, he instructed the attendants to take Mrs. Gilroy's coffin out to the cemetery. Six men dressed in somber black hoisted the simple casket to shoulder height. They descended the steps of the dais and walked solemnly toward the side doors of the church.

After the short graveside service, Hiram quietly prompted Margot toward the exit. Just as quietly, Margot insisted they stay, and followed the attendees as they started to file back into the church basement for refreshments. The other coffee ladies wanted to honor her in their way.

Despite feeling drained, Margot had to focus; coffee hour was the perfect opportunity to ask questions.

The area was brightly lit, with a dozen or so tables surrounded by mostly matching chairs. Three older women in white aprons over black dresses greeted them with sad smiles. They directed the attendees to tables in the front of the room. These were covered in white linens, with coffee services, teapots, and cups and saucers on one table, and an assortment of sliced cakes and cookies on the other.

She and Hiram made small talk with a few mourners, learning how each knew Mrs. Gilroy. None suggested any sort of nefarious business dealings with her. That was probably asking for a little too much. When her untouched coffee grew cold, Margot decided it was time to offer their condolences to Letitia and Calvin Jacobs, then depart.

The Jacobses sat at a square table, coffee and cake plates before them. Margot stepped closer, right hand extended. Hiram joined her.

"Mr. and Mrs. Jacobs, I'm Margot Harriman. This is Hiram Potter. Mrs. Gilroy worked for us, for my father, for many years. She was a lovely woman and will be sorely missed. I'm so very sorry for your loss."

Hiram offered his sympathies as well.

Mrs. Jacobs smiled as she took Margot's hand. She and Mrs. Gilroy were of similar coloring and features—nearly black hair going silver, gray eyes, pert nose. Alike enough to be sisters, though Mrs. Gilroy had been shorter and stouter.

"Yes, of course. Gia often spoke about you and the family. She always had some fun story to tell."

Margot smiled back, but her guilt blossomed once again. Mrs. Gilroy talked to her cousin about them? How had Margot let their relationship fade?

"She was an important part of the B&H family as well," Margot said with sincerity. She felt terrible that she had lost touch with Mrs. Gilroy.

"Gia was always going on about her work there, about how generous and kind you all were. I never quite understood what she did." Mrs. Jacobs's brow furrowed. "Some sort of secretary, wasn't it?"

"More of an assistant," Margot said. "She was crucial to my father especially."

No one had been able to keep Randolph on track like Mrs. Gilroy could, not since Margot's mother had passed a dozen years ago. And apparently Mrs. Gilroy was more involved with the goings-on at B&H than Margot had thought.

Mr. Jacobs cleared his throat. He was tall, even-seated, and more angular than his wife. His hangdog expression didn't seem to be from grief, though Margot assumed he was saddened by his cousin-in-law's passing to some extent.

"Do you know if she had a will?" he asked. "Used a lawyer at the company maybe?"

The question caught Margot by surprise, and she blinked at them for a moment before turning to Hiram.

"I'm not sure," he said. "Aren't there papers at her house?"

"Lettie and I haven't been there yet," Mr. Jacobs replied. "Didn't make it down until just before the service. A neighbor was kind enough to retrieve clothing for her for today."

Mrs. Jacobs shuddered. "Couldn't imagine staying in her house, under the circumstances. We're at our daughter and son-in-law's place. We'll be going over tomorrow to look for papers and see what family things she has, get the place ready to be cleaned up."

Alarm lurched painfully in Margot's chest. "Of course," she said.

Mrs. Jacobs continued to speak about several pieces she wanted to secure before having an estate sale. Her voice became background noise as Margot thought about papers and items stashed away, full of secrets waiting to be discovered. Secrets that could potentially ruin her and B&H.

They had to get into Mrs. Gilroy's house, and they had to do it tonight.

Eight

Hiram dropped Margot off at the steps of the Exeter Ladies Club on West 66th Street. She had made up a post-funeral luncheon date with an old school friend so Hiram wouldn't whisk her out of the city. To recuperate from the stress of the morning, she'd told him.

"Are you sure you don't want me to take you back to the house?" Hiram wasn't one for clubs or spending money when perfectly fine food waited at home.

Margot patted his hand. "I'm sure. I'll contact Bascom or find a cab." She grinned, resisting the urge to roll her eyes when he'd flinched at adding the cost of a cab to her expenses.

"I'm using my birthday money, Hiram, not putting it on the B&H account."

As if she didn't know better.

His cheeks flushed. "Don't be mean, Margot. I'll come by later to discuss the summer production schedule with you."

"Make it tomorrow morning, would you please?" It wasn't unusual for them to meet on a Saturday, particularly as the season was starting. She hoped she sounded innocent enough. "I don't think I'll be up for business this evening."

Or, if all went as planned, not at home for business this evening.

Hiram nodded, though he seemed a little put out. "All right. I'll call tomorrow at nine."

She exited his Model T and started up the stone stairs, taking her time. When she saw his vehicle turn the corner, she quickly descended the stairs, walking down the block to find a cab.

"Tenth and West Fifty-seventh," she said, giving the driver the nearest cross streets for Mancini & Associates.

The twelve-block drive took longer than Margot had hoped, but she was still over an hour early for the two o'clock appointment she'd arranged with Miss Mancini. Hopefully the up-and-coming private investigator was there.

She hurried up the front steps into the building, then up the interior stairs to the third floor. By the time she reached her destination, she was slightly winded.

Better get out and do some walking up and down hills, she thought as she raised her hand to knock. Muffled voices beyond the door caused her to hesitate.

A deep, gruff masculine one, loud but not clear enough to hear what was being said. Then a quieter, higher-pitched voice—Miss Mancini—attempted to mollify the other. The man's tone became louder, bordering on belligerent.

Unsure of what she could do to help, Margot rushed inside, nonetheless.

An older gentleman stood near Miss Mancini's desk, the brim of his fedora crumpled in his fisted hand, his back to Margot. Miss Mancini blocked the door to the inner office, the one marked PRIVATE.

"Mama is expecting you at home, Pop. You don't want to keep her waiting."

The man shook his head. "Don't tell me what to do!"

"Good afternoon," Margot called out.

Miss Mancini's gaze jumped to her, a mix of emotions crossing her features—surprise, embarrassment, perhaps relief. The gentleman whirled around, his face red with anger. Margot immediately saw the resemblance around their eyes and noses, though the man's hair had gone white.

"Who the blazes are you?" he demanded.

Miss Mancini stepped forward. "Pop, this is Miss Harriman. The lady I told you was coming in today."

Margot wasn't sure what Miss Mancini had told her father

about their arrangement, though she had said she'd discuss the case with him. Deciding it was best to keep their relationship vague for now, she entered the office, right hand extended. "How do you do, Mr. Mancini?"

Mr. Mancini's expression softened from anger to bewilderment to a bemused smile that seemed a bit forced as they shook hands. "Of course, of course, Miss Harriman. You've come to see me, then, have you?"

Margot and Miss Mancini exchanged glances.

"She's a friend of mine, Pop. We're headed to lunch. Mama said you should be home so your soup doesn't get cold." There was a hint of desperation in her eyes. Margot understood completely.

"It was a pleasure to meet you, sir," Margot said.

Albert Mancini nodded to her. He straightened the brim of his hat, set it on his head, and turned to Miss Mancini. "We'll see you Sunday for dinner, Loretta."

"I'll be there," she said, smiling. "Ciao, Pop. Kiss Mama for me."

Margot stepped out of the way to allow Mr. Mancini to pass. He left the office, carefully closing the door behind him.

Loretta Mancini crossed to her desk and sank down onto the chair. She scrubbed her palms over her face. When she looked up, her eyes held a weariness Margot had often seen staring back from her own mirror. "My apologies, Miss Harriman. I can explain."

"No need to, Miss Mancini." Margot sat on the same chair she'd occupied the other day. "There were times when my father was . . . not himself. If I wasn't around, either Mrs. Gilroy or Hiram Potter, our manager, took over as best they could. Most of the time, things went smoothly."

Randolph was generally easygoing, but now and again, particularly toward the end of his life, he'd burst into angry rants. Not that the shareholders thought any less of him—in public, at least. They'd have gladly continued with him at the helm, even as he was. But her? Only moderately capable in their minds.

"I never spoke to him about your case," Miss Mancini admitted, a blush rising on her cheeks.

Margot gave her an understanding smile. "I figured."

"If you decide to fire me, I can't blame you. I—"

"I have no intention of firing you. We all do what we need to do. When we first met, you made excuses for why your father wasn't in and who would be handling the case. I could see myself saying the same when Randolph was ill." The look of relief on Miss Mancini's face made Margot feel better as well. "I can empathize with what you're going through, Miss Mancini, but let's be straight with each other from here out. Now, aren't you going to ask me why I've arrived over an hour before our appointed time?"

The younger woman blinked at her, then glanced at the clock on a shelf. "Oh. You are early." Her demeanor changed, intensified. Business was at hand. "What happened at the funeral?"

Margot told her about Mrs. Gilroy's cousin Letitia and her husband going to the house the following day. "They'll be sorting through her things. I can't risk them finding something or destroying critical information out of ignorance. We need to see if Mrs. Gilroy left behind anything that might explain what she was trying to tell me in her note."

"Agreed." Miss Mancini leaned back in her chair, nodding thoughtfully, then sat forward again. "Wait. What do you mean 'we'? You can't be seen at her house."

"I won't be, if we go after dark."

Miss Mancini pressed her lips together, taking a moment before speaking with measured calmness. "Miss Harriman, do you have a key to Mrs. Gilroy's home?"

Margot couldn't help the bewilderment that surely showed on her face. "Well, no, of course not."

"No. Which means to get inside, we need to utilize certain methods and less than legal skills. Should we get caught, a woman of your social stature would be dragged through the mud, and the entire purpose of keeping this out of the public eye blown to bits."

Margot agreed with her there, but she had reasons for taking the risk. "Miss Mancini, I appreciate your concerns. I have them as well. But not only do I believe you can keep us from getting caught, I believe I can look over anything Mrs. Gilroy might have even vaguely related to the industry and evaluate it much more quickly than yourself. Also, I wish to be there and I am paying your fee. Now, do you have a way to get us into the house?"

"Yeah." Miss Mancini sighed in resignation and picked up the telephone. "I do."

NINE

Rett stood on the corner of a quiet street not too far from Saint Stephen's as the sun set over the East River. The few people who passed paid her little mind, save for a curious glance or two. She was obviously waiting for someone on the residential street, not plying the trade of a "working girl." That sort of activity could be found a few blocks south. Still, she hoped no one would remember her.

"Where's your client?" a soft alto queried at her right ear.

Rett jumped and whirled around, just stopping herself from snatching the brass knuckles out of her coat pocket. She should have expected Shiloh Wallace to be an ass.

The statuesque blonde wore black trousers, a striped

waistcoat, and an open-collared white shirt beneath a charcoal gray wool overcoat. The newsboy cap pulled low on her brow cast a shadow over her blue eyes and roman nose. Some would mistake her for a man even from up close, dressed as she was. If they saw her in her working clothes—a sparkling bodysuit and high heels—there would be no question of her feminine attributes.

"She'll be here soon. And what have I told you about sneaking up on me?" Rett closed her fist and held it up, shaking it in a mocking manner. "One of these days I'll end up giving you a knuckle sandwich and I won't be half sorry about it."

Shiloh laughed quietly. "Sorry, Rett. Comes with the job, ya know?"

As a magician's assistant and a hell of a prestidigitator herself, Shiloh had many skills that were useful off stage.

"Speaking of," the blonde continued, "have you been practicing?"

Rett patted the area of her left chest. "Got my set with me, but I'm not good enough yet for a door."

Shiloh shook her head, tsk-tsking disappointment. "Practice makes perfect, Loretta." Her gaze went past Rett, eyes bright in the light of the nearby streetlamp. "Is that your client?"

Rett turned around. Margot Harriman strolled down the street like she owned it. Even in plain, everyday clothes with a modest string of pearls around her neck, she couldn't hide the fact she was a woman who got what she wanted. Still, Miss Harriman's presence here ate at Rett.

"Yeah, that's her," she said with a sigh.

"Is she . . . ?" Shiloh's voice trailed off and she tilted her open hand back and forth, palm down.

"No. Well, I don't think so." Nothing Rett knew or heard about the food industry heiress and company president had ever indicated a relationship of any sort, actually. Definitely nothing that even hinted she preferred women. "Even if she is, she's off-limits. This isn't a social call, Shiloh, so please behave yourself."

Shiloh held up her hands. "Okay, but don't blame me if I get distracted. She's a looker."

She was at that, but while Rett could appreciate the beauty of other women, she was perfectly content with Cecelia.

Miss Harriman stopped in front of them, smiling. "Good evening." She held her right hand toward Shiloh. "I'm Margot."

Though they hadn't discussed using first names only, it was a smart move on Miss Harriman's part to do so.

Shiloh grinned, flashed a quick glance at Rett, then took the offered hand. "Shiloh. Nice to meet you."

"Interesting name," Miss Harriman said as they released each other's hands.

"My dad was into history."

Shiloh's dad was also into counterfeiting and forgery, but that was neither here nor there.

"Shall we?" Rett gestured down the street, toward Mrs. Gilroy's home two blocks away.

It was fully dark now, but they strolled causally, taking their time. Shiloh steered the conversation to theater productions and popular songs, while Rett kept an eye on other pedestrians who might appear too interested in them. There were few folks out walking that evening, thankfully.

When they were about half a block from the address, Rett spoke quietly. "Shiloh, go on ahead. Stay in the shadows best you can. The light over the stoop isn't on, and there are no lights on inside."

"Won't you need a light for your . . ." Miss Harriman made a vague gesture with one hand.

Shiloh scoffed as she withdrew her pick set from her coat pocket. "Please. I could do this blindfolded and underwater. In fact, I have."

She winked at Miss Harriman before sauntering up the brick steps to Mrs. Gilroy's door. Rett and Miss Harriman walked slowly toward the house. By the time they reached the bottom step, Shiloh had the door open and was waving them in. They hurried up the stairs and went inside, closing the door behind the three of them.

Rett took her flashlight out of her pocket—not the one with the brass knuckles—and flicked it on. Ghostly light and shadows danced in the foyer, illuminating the floral paper on the walls and a worn runner over hardwood. The short entryway opened to a small sitting area. A light aroma of roses hung in the air. A clock ticked somewhere. Nothing seemed to move in the otherwise silent house.

"Okay, Shiloh," Rett said. "I think we're good from here."

She hadn't told the woman why they needed to be inside, just that they had. Shiloh, being Shiloh, didn't ask too many questions.

"You sure?" The magician's assistant smiled at Miss Harriman. "I could stay and watch your backs or something."

Not that she didn't trust Shiloh to keep mum, but the fewer people who knew what they were doing, the better. Plus, it wasn't in Rett's interest to provide Shiloh with an object of affection.

"We'll be fine." Rett reached into her pocket for the fiver she'd brought for Shiloh. It wasn't there. There were no holes in the pocket. Had she dropped it when she took out the flashlight? She swept the beam of light along the floor. Nothing. Damn it.

"Looking for this?" Shiloh held up the bill.

"Did you find that on the floor or did you pick my pocket?"

The other woman grinned as she made the cash disappear. "What do you think?"

Miss Harriman chuckled.

Rett had to squelch her own laugh. "Got anything else to confess?"

The blonde dipped her hand into her coat pocket and withdrew a string of pearls.

Miss Harriman gasped, her hand immediately going to her bare throat.

"Sorry," Shiloh said, returning the necklace and not sounding sorry at all. "Habit. I would have given them back to you before I left."

Rett rolled her eyes. "Good night, Shiloh. And thanks."

"Say hi to Cecelia for me," Shiloh said, wagging her fingers before slipping out the door.

Rett threw the lock; it never hurt to be safe.

"You trust a lock-picking pickpocket not to talk about this?" Miss Harriman asked.

"I trust Shiloh *because* she is what she is. Not only is she a magician's assistant tasked with keeping her mouth shut about his tricks, she's been a good friend since eighth grade. She saved me from some neighborhood bullyboys, and I covered for her when one of the sisters was aiming to toss her from school."

Rett still got a chuckle over the fact that the daughter of a cop and the daughter of a criminal had become close. Most people didn't understand they were often two sides of the same demanding coin.

Miss Harriman stared at her for a few moments, mulling Rett's assurance, then nodded. "All right. If you trust her, I trust her. Let's get to this."

Rett led the way into the front room, keeping the flashlight beam low so it wouldn't be seen out the window. The same wallpaper covered these walls as in the entryway. The layout, furnishings, and rose scent reminded Rett of her nonna.

The room was pretty much what she expected an older widow would maintain. Overstuffed, heavy furniture, knick-knacks here and there, and grainy framed photographs of individuals and small groups of people. Rett picked up a photo of two young women and a boy of about ten wearing short pants and a crooked grin.

"That's Mrs. Gilroy," Miss Harriman said, coming up beside her. "On the left. I think the other young woman is her cousin Letitia."

"And the boy?"

"No idea. A relative of some sort, I'd imagine."

Rett put the photograph back on the sideboard.

The room lacked anything that looked like it might contain information about B&H, but Rett knew people were tricky.

"Have you ever visited here?" Rett asked. Maybe Miss Harriman had some idea of where her former employee stashed important items.

The longer than necessary silence from the other woman

had Rett turning around to make sure she'd heard the question. In the poor light, she caught what seemed to be sadness on Miss Harriman's face, but her expression shifted quick enough to make Rett unsure.

"No, I'd never visited Mrs. Gilroy."

Her tone had a definite hint of "let it go" to it.

"Okay. Look under and behind everything and anything," Rett suggested. "And wipe away any fingermarks you might leave."

"You've done this sort of thing before?" Miss Harriman sounded surprised.

"Let's just say I've gleaned a lot of information on technique over the years."

Leaving it at that, they searched the room, moving the settee, feeling under tables, lifting framed photos and paintings away from the walls. Nothing. The small kitchen had nothing to offer either, except for some food in the icebox that was starting to turn.

"Bedrooms?" Miss Harriman asked in a whisper.

Strange how being in the dark—and being in a home they had broken into—lent itself to quiet conversation.

Rett nodded and led the way down the hall. There were two bedrooms and a bathroom, all neat and clean. They looked through drawers and under the mattress in what appeared to be Mrs. Gilroy's room, but to no avail.

In the second bedroom, there was a narrow bed, a dresser

with a porcelain pitcher and bowl on top, and a secretary's desk.

Rett tried to lower the hinged front panel of the desk, but it was locked. "Hold the flashlight for me, would you?"

She handed the flashlight to Miss Harriman, who held the beam on the lock. Rett took her pick set out of her inner coat pocket.

"Why did we need Shiloh if you could do this?"

Rett bent over the lock and got to work. "I haven't graduated to doors yet. They tend to be more complicated."

"Oh."

She couldn't quite interpret Miss Harriman's response, but it made her grin anyway. Surely she didn't expect Rett to be a decent investigator as well as a completely law-abiding citizen. That rarely happened. Meeting Shiloh should have been more than enough of a clue.

The lock on the desk was simple and took her no more than a few seconds to open.

"Will you be able to relock it?"

Rett considered what that might entail. "Maybe. Probably."

"What about the front door when we leave?"

Damn it. She hadn't thought about that before sending Shiloh away. "I'll try. Worse comes to worst, the cousins will arrive tomorrow and think Mrs. Gilroy hadn't locked up behind her. But let's not get ahead of ourselves."

She lowered the front piece. The secretary had several

small drawers and pigeonholes. Stationery, pen, ink, blotters, blotter papers, all the expected accoutrements. There were several personal letters, bills, and other correspondence. Nothing about B&H or Randolph Harriman. Or any Harriman.

She opened the bottom right drawer. Inside was a navy blue, palm-sized, cloth-bound book with letters and numbers, pluses and minuses. Some of the sequences repeated.

"Why does she need a coded book?" Miss Harriman asked the same question Rett had been about to voice.

Rett flipped through the pages. The book was around two-thirds filled. She was about to close it when the back cover flopped down. There was a hard bulge beneath the back cover paper. Opening the book as wide as she could, she shook it. A small brass key fell onto the desk. She picked it up, holding it under the light. Numbers and letters were engraved along the length of it, but no other identifying marks.

"What might it go to?" Miss Harriman asked.

"Something small. Another desk?" Rett suggested.

"A strongbox?" Miss Harriman countered. "Or a safety-deposit box?"

Rett's gaze fell upon the stack of correspondence. There were several pieces from the J. Ferrier Bank and Trust, a few more from the New York Bank of the Bronx. No other financial institutions she could discern. "We'll need to check. Let's take a look at these and—"

The sound of the front door rattling stopped her. It wasn't a loud sound, but there had been no other noises in the house.

"Hide," Rett whispered fiercely.

She pocketed the book and key and shut off the flashlight as Miss Harriman dashed behind the dresser. She quietly shut the front piece of the secretary and tiptoe-hurried behind the open door. Listening as the footsteps drew closer, she watched through the narrow space between the door and the jamb.

A shadowed figure approached, flashlight beam held low. A largish man, from what she could tell of his heavy gait and form. He turned toward the room she and Miss Harriman occupied, like he knew exactly where to go.

The man entered. Rett slid her left hand into the pocket with her brass knuckles and pushed her fingers through the rings. She readied her metal-enhanced fist as the man's beam of light swept through the room. He moved the door, exposing her. Rett's heart pounded, about to jump out of her chest. *Damn, damn, damn.*

The light arced across her feet, then up toward her face.

"What the—"

As Rett cocked her arm, fist tight around the knuckleduster, a crash and thump cut him off.

The man dropped like a sack of wet mud, his flashlight rolling out of his hand.

Rett fumbled for her light and raised it to Miss Harriman's stunned face. She held the broken handle of the pitcher that had been on the dresser. The rest of it was in pieces around the downed man.

"I—I panicked," she stammered.

"You did fine." Rett played her beam of light over the man. He was brown-haired with thick russet stubble shadowing his cheeks. Rather ordinary in appearance. She knelt and checked for a pulse in his neck. Still alive. That was a relief. Patting his coat pockets in search of a wallet, she felt something hard. Rett reached in. Her fingers wrapped around the cool metal of what could only be a revolver. Shit. That could have been bad. Very bad. She left the weapon there and stood.

There were more immediate concerns.

"Recognize him? Was he at the funeral?"

"Not that I recall." Miss Harriman used her skirt to wipe fingermarks from the pitcher handle. "He's not dead, is he?"

"No, but he's going to have a hell of a headache. Come on. We need to skedaddle."

They hurried back through the house. Before opening the door, Rett checked if anyone was outside. No one she could see, though if there was a lookout for the man hiding somewhere, they *wouldn't* see him, would they? At least the darkness provided some cover for their identities as well. And there was no need for them to worry about locking the door behind them. It was that guy's problem now.

Rett covered her hand with the front of her coat, preventing fingermarks as she opened then shut the front door behind them. They scurried down the steps and away from the house, keeping their pace purposeful but casual. Surely Miss Harriman's heart was racing as fast as her own.

"I didn't expect to add assault to my criminal activities," Miss Harriman said.

Rett tried not to laugh. "That was quick thinking with the pitcher, Miss Harriman."

As they turned a corner, she let out a sigh. "We just broke into a dead woman's home, stole from her, and clobbered a man. I think you can call me Margot, Loretta."

Rett did chuckle at that, releasing her own nervousness. "Fair enough. And it's Rett to my friends."

In the yellow light of the streetlamp they passed, Margot smiled. There was something in her eyes then, a softening, and a glint that Rett couldn't quite grasp the meaning of before they were back in the shadows. "Rett, then. Let's find a cab."

TEN

Margot stepped down from the carriage with help from the driver. Long skirts were so very awkward in these situations. Her mind skipped to Shiloh in her trousers and cap. Wouldn't it be lovely if she could get away with that?

Once she had her feet beneath her, she glanced around Rett's neighborhood. Although only a few streetlights burned, the buildings seemed in good repair. No one was about. Somewhere down the road a dog barked and a man yelled for it to shut up. The damp spring air made her shiver, and Margot regretted only having her lighter coat.

She opened her purse as the driver gave Rett a hand. By

the time he turned to her, Margot had dug out a few coins to cover the fee and a tip.

"Thanks," he said. "Anything else for you ladies?"

Margot held up a couple of half dollar coins. "Can you return in an hour, um . . . ?"

He smiled. "Harvey, ma'am. And yes, ma'am, I certainly can."

"Excellent." She handed him the coins. "Thank you, Harvey. See you then."

He tipped his hat to them and swung back up into the driver's seat. With a click of his tongue and a gentle flick of the reins, he set off.

"Money sure does talk," Rett said.

"Sometimes louder than deserved," she said dryly.

Rett started up the steps of a narrow apartment building. "Could've stayed the night. We'd set you up on the divan with a pillow and blanket."

Margot couldn't quite tell if she was joking.

At the top of the stairs, Rett produced a ring of keys from her pocket. She unlocked the front door and held it open for Margot. There was a lamp on a table in the foyer, under a boxy telephone with a crank on the side. Stairs led up to the other four floors.

After locking the door behind them, Rett came to Margot's side. "We're up on three. No elevator. Sorry."

Had she expected Margot to balk at taking the stairs? She waved off Rett's unnecessary apology. "Lead on."

They climbed the stairs without much conversation, for which Margot was grateful. As much as she hated people assuming she was weak, she really needed to get out walking more often.

She followed Rett down the hall, a worn runner muting their footfalls. Several lamps hung from the ceiling, frosted glass globes softening the light.

"Here we are," Rett said stopping in front of a scarred wood door marked 3C. "Cecelia, my, uh, roommate, will be at work so we won't be bothered."

She unlocked the door and stood aside to allow Margot in.

"Is your roommate generally a bother?" Margot asked, smiling.

Luckily, Rett understood her quip and grinned back. "Not at all. CeeCee is inquisitive, but also discreet. One of the reasons we get along so well."

Margot went inside and Rett followed, shutting the door behind them. The apartment was small, neat, and homey. The kitchen area and sitting room were one space, with a short hallway that Margot assumed led to a bedroom or two and perhaps a bathroom.

"Make yourself comfortable," Rett said as she took Margot's coat. "I'll get us some tea."

She handed Margot the book, key, and papers they'd taken from Mrs. Gilroy's house. Margot brought them into the sitting room, sat on the floral-upholstered love seat, and skimmed the book while Rett puttered about the kitchen. The notations made no sense, but there had to be a pattern of some sort.

"What does your roommate do?" Margot asked.

"She's a night nurse at City Hospital. Taking medical classes during the day."

Margot looked up in surprise. "She's studying to be a doctor? Fantastic. We need more women in that field."

These young women impressed her.

"We think so too." Rett came in with a tray that held cups but no teapot. "Water's heating up. Did you find anything in the book?"

Margot handed the slim volume and key back to Rett. "Not really. I'd wager a code of some sort, likely regarding deposit dates and amounts, if the key with it goes to a safety-deposit box."

Rett squinted down at the small brass key. "Some numbers and letters on it, but nothing else. As you said, probably a lock or safety-deposit box key. But for which bank? There were papers from two. And neither are close enough to Mrs. Gilroy's to be a 'neighborhood' bank."

Something tickled the edge of Margot's memories. "I think Mrs. Gilroy's late husband worked at J. Ferrier Bank and Trust."

"Interesting," Rett said as she put the book and key down. "I'll go to the banks next week, if you can put off my employment at the cannery for a few days."

"Easy enough." Margot tapped the key. "How will you figure out where this goes to?"

"I'll go into each New York branch and rent a safety-deposit box. Comparing the keys should tell us which bank. If it's one of them. Fingers crossed there isn't a different bank involved."

Comparing keys made sense, but there was still a slight hitch.

"You can't open an account on your own."

That women weren't permitted to have their own private accounts rankled.

Rett headed into the kitchen to fix the tea. "True, but I have an idea."

"Anything I can do?" Margot didn't want to overstep, but she felt the need to offer some assistance where she could. "If you're opening an account, you'll need money."

"That would be helpful. And you're doing plenty." Rett had her back to Margot. "I mean, you hired me to do this so you wouldn't risk anyone knowing you were looking into something, right?"

Was Rett rebuking her for accompanying her this evening? Margot bit back the instinct to respond, keeping the defense of her actions to herself. "I did."

Rett turned around, teapot wrapped in a towel, and came toward her. "I appreciate that you—"

Before she could continue, the door opened and a plump blonde in nurse's whites strode in. "Hi, how'd it go, swee—Oh!" Her blue eyes found Margot's and she smiled politely. "Hello."

Rett put the teapot down. "Margot, this is my roommate, Cecelia. CeeCee, this is Margot."

Margot rose and extended her right hand. "How do you do?"

The other woman crossed the short span of the room and they shook hands. Cecelia's was dry and rough but warm. Hard work and constant washing as a nurse accounted for their condition, contrary to Margot's more privileged position.

She watched for any indication that the woman knew who she was. Had Rett betrayed her privacy? She'd sworn not to, and Shiloh hadn't seemed to know who she was earlier, but roommates tended to chat.

For all Margot could tell, Cecelia appeared to think nothing at all of her appearance at their apartment. Nor interested in her identity. Margot's trust and confidence in Rett Mancini went up a notch.

"I'll get you some tea," Rett offered.

"I've got some studying to do. That's why I'm home early. It was quiet on the floor, so Mrs. Beatty let me go, knowing I have a test coming up." She unpinned her cap. "I'll take a cup into, um, my room, if that's okay. Lovely to meet you, Margot."

"Likewise," Margot said. "Good luck on your test."

Rett handed Cecelia one of the filled teacups and saucers.

They smiled at each other before Cecelia headed down the hall. A door closed quietly.

"Sorry about that," Rett said.

"No need to apologize. This is her home. I'm sure she works hard and deserves what time she can get."

"You've got that right." Rett glanced down the hall, grinning. She turned back to Margot. "I suppose we shouldn't discuss things though, now that CeeCee is here. She's no squealer or gossip, I assure you, but I wouldn't want to make you uncomfortable."

Margot sipped her tea. "I appreciate that. I believe you have the situation well in hand for Monday. I'll have the cash delivered to your office first thing."

Rett nodded. "There are a few details to get straight, but those shouldn't be a problem. I can call you Monday evening to give you an update."

"I'll go back through the files Randolph kept at the house. There may be something I missed, something related to either of the banks."

If her father had personal or business accounts at J. Ferrier Bank and Trust or the New York Bank of the Bronx, shouldn't Margot know about them? Something else he could have been keeping from her.

The tea did nothing to alleviate the bitterness biting at the back of her throat.

Eleven

Rett looped her arm through Daniel Boone Wallace's as they strode up the street toward the J. Ferrier Bank and Trust. Shiloh's younger brother rested his hand on top of hers, flashing her a charming smile and a wink. She gazed up at him with the same smile, putting her acting skills to the test. She liked Danny well enough, and trusted him with this ruse, but that was as far as it went.

Their first stop earlier that Monday morning at the more middle class–serving New York Bank of the Bronx hadn't panned out. That establishment didn't offer safety-deposit boxes, so they couldn't test the key found in Mrs. Gilroy's desk. If Mrs. Gilroy had used an account there for something other than personal business, they'd have to figure out something else. Rett crossed her fingers and toes on that one.

"Lots of swells around here," she said, noting the extravagant hats on the ladies.

Her own modest headwear didn't hold a candle to some of the feathered pieces bobbing in the breeze. Rett felt a little out of place, though she wore her best dress and Danny had on a good suit. The style and price tag of the pedestrians' garb rose as they had traveled from the streetcar stop.

Danny smiled at an older couple as they passed. "After our business is complete perhaps we can partake in some luncheon."

Rett shook her head and rolled her eyes, hoping the "swanky" accent he used didn't sound as silly to other ears. "Knock it off, Danny. Stay in character."

Though he was an actor, Danny's main income came from tending bar and the three-card monte con he ran in Times Square when he wasn't working small jobs for his father and learning the family business. Folks passing by on their way to and from the theater were his favorite marks.

His handsome face, so like Shiloh's they could have been twins, turned sober and serious. "Yes, ma'am. But honestly, Rett, I could use a bite. Didn't get breakfast this mornin'."

"Fine," Rett said with a sigh. "I'll buy you coffee and a sandwich when we're done here."

He grinned and opened one of the double doors for her. "Peachy. After you, my dear."

The interior of the J. Farrier Bank and Trust was all rich woods, shiny brass, and green-veined white marble floor. Everything from the long counter separating the customers from the tellers to the tellers themselves was crisp and clean, though the place smelled of old money and cigars. The conversation among the predominantly male occupants was at an almost church-level hush, as if the confines of their world was something sacred.

The uniformed security guard at the door quirked a bushy gray eyebrow at them. "Can I help you?"

Rett smiled demurely as Danny swept his hat off his head. "Indeed," he said. "We're looking to open an account. Can we see someone about that, please?"

The guard gave them a quick perusal. "Minimum deposit here is one hundred dollars. You have that much?"

Danny stiffened. The grin on his face collapsed into a frown. "I don't discuss financial affairs with glorified doormen."

The guard scowled. "Listen, you . . ."

Rett squeezed Danny's arm. If he blew this for her, she was going to break his limb. "Now, dear, he was just trying to make sure we were in the right place." She raised her voice a little when she saw a well-dressed man come toward them from behind a desk. "I'm sure we can talk to someone who will help us."

"Is there some sort of problem, Mr. Jenkins?" The man from the desk smiled tightly at Rett and Danny, unsure of them himself, it seemed. He smoothed a lock of gray hair from his forehead.

The guard placed his hands on his hips. "No problem, Mr. Pace. These folks are looking to open an account. I was informing them of the bank minimum. To save them trouble."

Despite wearing their Sunday best, it seemed Jenkins didn't believe she and Danny had enough money to be inside the bank, let alone open an account. Luckily, Margot had supplied them with sufficient cash. But still, who were they to judge if someone was "worthy" to even come into their stinking bank?

If she could have, Rett would have given Pace and the guard a piece of her mind. Unfortunately, they needed to get past the front door, and then some.

"Never you mind. Mr. Pace, is it?" Rett smiled at the gentleman. "We want to put our *inheritance* in a safe and reputable place, is all."

Her emphasis on the word made Mr. Pace's lips twitch as if he could taste the cash. Excellent.

Danny set his hat upon his head again and gave the men a curt nod. "Though that may not be here. Come along, dear."

Rett gently resisted his attempt to turn her around. *Damn it, Danny, I will kill you.*

"Please, wait a moment," Pace said, holding his hands

out in supplication. Rett was almost giddy with relief that he'd stopped them. "I apologize for Mr. Jenkins's behavior." He shot a glare at the guard. "Come sit down, Mister and Missus . . . ?"

Danny kept the disgruntled expression on his face. "Walters. Daniel and Lor—" Rett squeezed his arm again. "Loreen Walters."

Pace's smile grew and he held his right hand out. "A pleasure to meet you both. I'm Francis Pace." He shook their hands then gestured toward the direction he'd come. "Please, let's have a seat and we'll see what J. Ferrier can do for you."

They followed Pace to his desk near the rear corner of the bank, not far from the counter of tellers and customers. The ornately carved desk had several ledgers and folders on it, as well as a blotter and a silver-plated pen-and-ink set. As Danny waited for her to take one of the upholstered chairs, Rett noticed the door just beyond Pace's desk.

"Let's get some initial information, shall we?" Pace took his seat, opened a drawer, and withdrew several pieces of paper. He plucked a silver and black pen from the set and looked up at Danny expectantly. "Full name?"

Danny provided Pace with the information he and Rett had created. Close enough to the truth, but not true enough to be traced back to them.

"Make sure Loreen is on the account," Danny said, tapping the desk. "The missus needs access to it, as I travel a lot."

"Of course, Mr. Walters." The banker flashed Rett a smile and jotted down her name. "Do you have some sort of identification? An employment card, perhaps?"

Rett kept her expression neutral, but her heart thudded hard. Still, she noted Pace didn't ask her for any such thing.

Without hesitation, Danny reached into the inside pocket of his jacket and withdrew a leather wallet. He opened it and removed a white card. "Been at Harris Property Managers for near on six years. Good folks."

He handed the card to Pace. From what Rett had seen earlier when they were concocting their identities as the Walters, it was properly worn around the edges, as if it had lived in Danny's wallet for those six years. The advantages of being related to a top-notch forger and counterfeiter. "Daniel Walters" had existed even before Rett needed him to.

"Ah, very good." Pace jotted down information from the card and gave it back to Danny. He turned the paper around to face them and held out a pen. "Your signatures, please. We'll check those as well when withdrawals are requested."

Danny and Rett each signed.

Pace opened one of his tabbed ledgers to a section marked "W" and wrote in their names. His pen hovered over a column. "And how much are you depositing today?"

"One hundred and fifty dollars," Danny said.

"And we'd like to rent a safety-deposit box." Rett smiled shyly. "I have some of my mother's jewelry."

Pace went back into the drawer for another piece of paper. "Of course. Box rental is one dollar per month. We can take it out of your account automatically."

Danny's eyebrows shot up. "A dollar? That seems a wee bit steep for a box you keep locked in a vault anyway."

Rett had to refrain from smacking him. "Dear, it's important."

Pace's chin rose slightly. "I assure you, Mr. Walters, the security of your most precious items is as crucial to us as your money is to you. Surely knowing your mother-in-law's jewelry is surrounded by thick steel and protected by our rigorous process is worth such a nominal fee."

Rett cocked her head. "How rigorous, Mr. Pace?"

If the bank used a two-key process to access individual boxes, they were in trouble.

Pace sat up straighter, pride and confidence clear on his smooth face. "We use a code word system as well as the signature comparison. And only two managers have access to the necessary books and keys, myself and Mr. Gates."

Rett and Danny exchanged looks. "I suppose that'll do," she said.

The banker's smile turned brittle for a second. "I'm

so glad. Do you have the funds for your new account deposit?"

"Of course." Rett dug into her purse and withdrew the plain brown envelope Margot had sent her. She handed it to Pace, the glint of the borrowed gold ring on her finger catching her eye. Such a strange sensation, having it there. "One hundred and fifty dollars. It's everything inherited from Papa. We want to have something for our children."

Rett laid her palm flat on her stomach and tried to beam, though the thought of having a kid made her feel the exact opposite.

Pace's face brightened. "Well! Congratulations!"

He reached out to shake Danny's hand again. Danny nodded, a bit of a self-congratulatory smirk on his face. Rett wanted to slap both of them, but she played along.

With the cash counted and noted in the ledger, Pace excused himself while he went behind the counter to speak to a teller. The younger man nodded and put the cash into a locked drawer. The cash would be secured in the vault later, as was standard practice at the end of the day. Once they were done with the case, she and Danny would return to close out the account and get Margot's money back to her.

Pace crossed back to a wooden cabinet near his desk, opening it with one of the many keys on a ring kept in his pocket. Inside the cabinet was a small metal box that also required a key. He made notes in yet another book then pocketed something before returning to his desk.

He handed the open book to Danny. "If you'd be so kind as to write down your code word beneath your name."

Rett watched Danny write "Brooklyn Dodgers" then hand the book back to Pace.

"Follow me, please," he said, "and we can get your personal items secured."

Rett and Danny followed Pace past the tellers' counter and through the unmarked door, which he had to unlock and then lock behind them. She hoped this was the right bank; she couldn't imagine having to open accounts and rent boxes all over town. The paneled corridor leading to the rear of the building smelled of wood oil and tobacco smoke, with doors on either side and another corridor branching to the right. Pace turned down the side hall. A large steel door marked the end of that path.

Another key from Pace's ring, the largest this time, opened the steel door that led to a cage-lined room. There was an even larger, more formidable steel door here, one with a spoked handle and a numbered dial.

"As you can see," Pace said, "it requires several keys and a combination to access the safety-deposit boxes."

"Yes, very impressive." Danny nodded in approval.

Pace moved forward, blocking the dial with his body, lest she or Danny figure out the combination. The click-click-

click of the mechanism meant nothing to Rett, but when she glanced at Danny, she noticed his intense stare at Pace's back. She nudged Danny, eyes widening in a way that clearly said, "Knock it off!"

"You made me lose count," he whispered.

"You're not here to case the joint," she whispered back.

"What was that?" Pace glanced over his shoulder as he spun the handle and pulled the door open.

"I said I'm counting on your top-notch security to keep the missus happy."

Pace grinned back. "Come in, please."

Danny's eyes lit up, but he was soon harrumphing in disappointment, as if he'd expected to see stacks of cash or piles of gold.

A polished wood and iron table sat in the center of the vault for patrons to sort the contents of their boxes. The two side walls were lined with numbered panels, each with a keyhole. The back wall was yet another solid-looking steel door.

Pace held a key out to Danny. Rett's heart quickened. It was identical to the one they had taken from Mrs. Gilroy's house, which was currently burning a proverbial hole in her purse.

"Your box is number eighty-four, there on the right," Pace said. "I'll step outside and close the door, but rest assured you aren't locked in."

"We won't be long," Danny said.

The banker gave them a slight bow and left the secured room.

Rett put her purse on the table while Danny went to the wall of boxes. "What's the number on the key?" she asked.

He squinted down at the engraved brass. "Looks like . . . C Four Three."

The engraving on Mrs. Gilroy's key read K2-2.

Rett took a notebook and pencil out of her purse and drew a sketch of the safety-deposit boxes. Three rows of smaller boxes in six columns over three rows of four columns of larger boxes made up one of three sections on one wall. The opposite wall held the same configuration, for one hundred and eight boxes on each wall, or two hundred and sixteen boxes in total.

Chewing lightly on the end of the pencil, she considered their key code and the box number assigned. "Depending on how they assigned the letter designation . . ."

"The K section is either on the bottom center of the right wall or on the top right. Probably," Danny finished for her.

Rett's head came up. He was standing beside her, peering down at her hasty sketch. "You figured that out that quickly?"

He shrugged. "It's a gift." Then, giving her the dazzling Wallace smile, said, "That helps with the grift."

She laughed. Returning her attention to the sketch, she tapped their assigned box. "If you go down four and over three, you get our eighty-four."

Danny straightened up and faced one of the walls. "So that means the one we're looking for is . . ." He counted boxes in the bottom center section. "Here."

Rett inserted Mrs. Gilroy's key into the lock. There was a moment of slight resistance, then it turned.

"Brilliant," Danny said over her shoulder.

She opened the door. Inside was a metal box that, luckily, had no locking mechanism. Rett brought it out and set it on the table, anticipation welling like a kid at Christmas. Danny stood across from her. She didn't want to let him in on what was inside, but he was right there and had done so much to help. And it wasn't as if she would go into detail.

Rett lifted the lid. "Holy Hannah."

Danny let out a low whistle of appreciation.

Two-inch-thick stacks of banknotes, neatly secured by rubber bands, sat atop a brown envelope. Rett slid the envelope from under the cash. There were no markings on it, but it contained sheets of paper. She turned away to keep Danny's nose from peeking and slid the pages partially out of the envelope. Damn it. More coded copy, but these looked like invoices of some sort. Materials? Payments for services?

Where was the decoder, if there was one? If Mrs. Gilroy kept it in her head, they were done.

Rett put the envelope in her purse. It barely fit, even when she folded it.

"How much is there, do you think?" Danny asked.

"Let's find out." She handed him one of the stacks. "You are to count. Do not pocket a single note. Understand?"

He looked appropriately, if insincerely, shocked by her implications. "Of course."

When they were finished, the notes totaled over two thousand dollars in ten- and twenty-dollar denominations. That was . . . significant.

Rett secured the band around her stack and put it in the box. Why would Giana Gilroy have so much cash in a safety-deposit box? If it was hers, wouldn't an account suffice? Hopefully, whatever was in the envelope would explain.

"Okay, let's put this back and get out of here."

Danny banded his stack and handed it to her. Rett gave him a questioning look. He crossed his heart and held up three fingers like a Boy Scout. "Not a note, I swear."

She returned the box to its slot and the key to her purse. Danny opened the vault door. Mr. Pace stood at the end of the short hall, speaking to a young man as they looked over several sheets of paper. Both abruptly stopped talking when Rett and Danny came out.

"We'll discuss this later," Pace said, patting the man on the shoulder and gesturing toward the door leading back to the main room of the bank.

The young man glanced nervously at Rett and Danny. She didn't recognize him. Did he know her or Danny? Danny didn't show anything, but then again, he could be very much the professional. If he knew the man, he'd let her know.

Pace turned to Rett and Danny, smiling. "All done, then?"

"Yes, thanks." Danny put his arm around Rett's shoulder as they moved aside to let Pace lock the vault door.

"Is there anything else I can do for you?" he asked.

Rett and Danny exchanged looks, shaking their heads slightly. When she turned to tell Pace there was nothing else, she noticed him staring at her purse. Rett swallowed hard. Was the envelope sticking out? Was there something on it or about it she had missed? She didn't dare draw attention to it. Instead she smiled and nudged Danny.

"Nothing I can think of, thank you, Mr. Pace," Danny said.

Pace met her gaze and smiled. "Let me show you out."

He led them back through the bank to the foyer. Jenkins, the guard, gave them a glare, then resumed his watch over the quiet activities of the J. Ferrier Bank and Trust. Pace shook each of their hands and bade them good day, thanking them for their business and looking forward to seeing them soon. Rett was sure they wouldn't be back, except to withdraw Margot's money and return the box key.

Danny opened the door for her and stood aside for Rett to exit. The cool spring day had her drawing her coat tighter around herself. She checked that the envelope was still secure in her purse, then she took Danny's arm.

Now that they had access to Mrs. Gilroy's box and the papers, all Rett wanted to do was get the hell out of there.

"Mr. and Mrs. Walters, wait!"

Rett's heart jumped to her throat hearing Mr. Pace calling for them. Her immediate instinct was to bolt. Danny held her back.

"Easy," he muttered. "Guilty people run. We ain't done nothin'. Just turn around."

Unless Pace had recognized the envelope in her purse.

She allowed Danny to guide her around to face Mr. Pace. He strolled toward them, holding up a small green book.

"You forgot your account book," he said, smiling.

Danny grinned back. "Ah, thank you. Wouldn't want anyone getting hold of our information or money, would we?"

He took the offered booklet and slipped it into his jacket pocket.

"Again, I assure you that your money is safe as can be at J. Ferrier. No one has access to anything but their own belongings and money."

Considering what she and Danny had just accomplished, Rett fought to hold back a laugh.

"Good to know." Danny tipped his hat. "Thank you, sir. Good day."

Pace nodded to each of them. "Good day."

He turned and strode back inside.

Rett turned Danny around, nearly pulling him down the

sidewalk, her heart thumping and sweat dampening the crown of her head beneath her hat.

"Slow down there, Rett," Danny said. "Unless you're racing to catch the last bowl of soup at Monty's, that is."

Rett took a breath and laughed. She settled into a normal gait to keep up with Danny's longer stride. "Right. Lunch. I suppose I can swing more than coffee and a sandwich. Come on."

TWELVE

Margot blew an errant lock of hair out of her mouth and swiped perspiration off her forehead with the back of her hand. The basement was cool enough, but moving around old boxes of files certainly worked up a sweat. Her stomach grumbled. And hunger, apparently.

She had dived into the old company files stored at home. Reams of paper pertaining to financial reports, loans, and payments. So far, nothing unusual or associated with unfamiliar financial institutions had cropped up. Seeing her mother's name or that of her grandparents had made Margot smile even as grief fluttered in her chest, but no items seemed connected to nefarious deeds. If there was nothing here, could there be something at the cannery? Or in another location? How would they ever find it?

"Miss Harriman?" Caroline called from the top of the stairs.

"Just a minute!" Margot shoved boxes back into their rows and gave the collection a final glare. She hadn't gone through all of them, but she wasn't anticipating sudden success. She started up the stairs. "Yes?"

Caroline, in her neat black dress and pristine apron, pressed her lips together as she appraised Margot's condition. "Miss Mancini is here."

Damn it. It was later than Margot realized.

"Right. I'll change and wash up. Extend my apologies for my delay and give her a drink, would you?" She headed toward the back stairs. "Something strong."

"Yes, miss."

Margot hurried up to her room. A quick glance in the vanity mirror showed her less disheveled than she feared, but there was a fair amount of dust on her face and hair, and her dress was smudged with grime up the sleeves. Stripping as quickly as she could, she soaked a cloth in the bathroom sink and wiped her face and arms. It wasn't perfect, but it would do.

She returned to her bedroom and took a simple blouse and skirt from the closet. Not her typical attire for supper. Rett Mancini wouldn't care. Truth be told, neither did she.

A final check in the mirror, a quick pin to a strand of hair, and Margot went back downstairs. She found Rett in the parlor sipping what appeared to be whisky from a heavy glass.

"Hello, Rett. Sorry to keep you waiting."

Rett stood as Margot joined her and poured herself a couple of fingers of liquor from the decanter on the coffee table.

"Not a problem," Rett said. "I have news."

Margot gestured for her to take her seat once again, noticing the crud under her own fingernails, and settled in the chair opposite her.

"You were successful at the bank?" Margot raised her glass to Rett when she nodded, though they were too far apart for a proper toast.

"To a degree, yes. There are still more questions." Rett put her glass on the table. She opened her purse and withdrew a plain brown envelope, handing it to Margot. "Along with over two thousand dollars in cash, there was this."

"Two thousand dollars in cash?" The amount was stunning, to say the least. What had Mrs. Gilroy been doing to have that much hidden away?

Margot opened the envelope. The first page was a list of dates and corresponding numbers. Most of the numbers were the same for each, with the dates spaced every month over the course of two years. The most recent notation was last month.

"A regular payment of some sort," she said.

"Yes, but for what?" Rett gestured to the second page.

"That one is similar, but the dates are more regular. The same amount on the twenty-fifth of each month for over two years."

"And like the first list, still being paid as of last month. The question is, to whom and for what?" What did that cash and these notations have to do with B&H? Her stomach tightened at the thought of money going out she didn't know about, for reasons that were likely less than legal.

Rett tapped the rim of her glass. "What sort of regular expenses does B&H have?"

Margot blew out a breath as the list formed in her head. "Plenty. Payroll, electricity, water, vehicle leasing. There are also food and ingredients deliveries like flour, sugar, and salt to our bakery. Paper and printing for labels, canning materials. That's just off the top of my head."

"The legitimate ones." Rett said with a wry grin. "I think we're looking for something less on the up-and-up."

"Mmm." Margot nodded, her thoughts churning. "Payoffs. Blackmail."

"Exactly." Rett sorted through the papers, brow furrowed, and asked, "Why?" Her tone was more speculative than probing.

Margot focused on the younger woman. "Why what?"

"Why did your Mrs. Gilroy keep those records at all? If they're illegal payments of some sort, which I think we can assume they are, why note it? Why not just pay and leave no trail?"

Margot couldn't help but smile. "Mrs. Gilroy preferred to have everything just so, a perfect balance to my father's more random and distracted personality. It doesn't surprise me that even when it came to things they ought not be doing, Mrs. Gilroy was as organized and precise as ever. I don't think she could have been otherwise."

"Some habits are hard to break. Which could be in our favor. Records kept means records to be found."

"Yes, but"—Margot held up the pages—"if we can't determine what those records are saying, they're rather pointless."

Rett sipped her drink. "We need a decoder."

Easier said than done.

"I'm not friendly with any cipher experts. Are you?" Margot asked.

The younger woman's expression clouded. "No, but that doesn't mean we can't figure it out."

Margot felt her throat tighten a bit. "How long might that take?"

"No idea," Rett admitted, "though we can't let that deter us."

Margot was sure to keep her voice calm, despite the thought now racing in her mind. She stood and smoothed her skirt. "I'll keep looking through old records. Maybe something will pop up."

But if not, they'd be no further along.

Rett eyed Margot. "You're a hard one to read. But I can still tell there's something more on your mind."

Margot drew a slow breath, weighing whether to share her concerns with Rett. The younger woman held her gaze, waiting for Margot to continue. Of course she had to confide in Rett about her fears. That's why she'd been hired, but more important, there was a ticking clock now.

"The payments had been made regularly for two years. Up until the twenty-fifth of last month. We're into the fourth week of April, and Mrs. Gilroy is dead."

Understanding dawned in Rett's eyes. "The twenty-fifth is in three days. What happens when the next payment isn't met?"

"I'd imagine that whoever doesn't get the money will do, or not do, something that will end up hurting B&H." Margot's stomach churned. Everything she and her family had worked for, threatened by secrets and lies.

"How are you supposed to make a payment to someone if you don't know who is being paid?"

The bitter laugh that escaped Margot was nearly accompanied by a sob, but she caught herself just in time. She couldn't let Rett see her falter. "An excellent question."

Rett also got to her feet. "Chances are your extortionist will know Mrs. Gilroy is dead. They might hold off on spilling the beans or whatever until they're sure the cash flow is cut off."

Margot narrowed her gaze at the other woman. "I'm not quite sure if that makes me feel better or worse."

"Yeah, I don't know either," Rett said, wincing, "but it might mean we have a little time. Most people won't just throw in the towel on a good thing, and holding something over a big company willing to continue payoffs would be considered a good thing."

It was Margot's turn to wince. "Wonderful."

Rett patted her arm reassuringly. "We'll figure this out, Margot."

She paused for a moment, a curious look in her eyes.

"What are you thinking?" Margot asked.

"Why was Mrs. Gilroy in Julia Blumfeld's office?"

"I'm not sure." Margot wondered the same thing, but couldn't figure it out. "Perhaps she wanted Julia to find the note for me?"

"If she hadn't passed away," Rett said, "she would have addressed it to you and probably left it there on Julia's desk. Why not leave it at the reception desk downstairs?"

"She and Julia got along well. I'm sure she trusted Julia to give the note to me without any fuss or question."

Rett tilted her head slightly. "Were there people in the cannery she didn't get on with? Someone she wouldn't trust with the note?"

A frisson of uneasiness traveled up Margot's spine. "Are you suggesting someone may have meant her harm? The coroner said it was a natural death."

"I don't know. But why go to Julia's office? Why not come

here or, since she had keys, leave the note in Potter's or another office?"

The question stumped Margot. "Do you think it's important?"

"Could be. She may have had a reason for being at the cannery. Nostalgia? But I'm more inclined to think otherwise."

She didn't want to read too much into the situation, but Margot's own curiosity got the better of her. "What *do* you think?"

Rett gave Margot a look she had come to associate with the investigator's cool intensity. "Something or someone prompted her to pick *that* day and *that* time to go to B&H. To choose *that* manner of communicating with you. It may have been personal, but there was a reason. Maybe if we figure out that reason, we can figure out what's been going on."

Thirteen

"What's going on in there, a party?" From the doorway, cannery supervisor Ken Thorpe's deep voice echoed against the light blue walls and colorful doors of the B&H ladies' locker room. "We got carrots and potatoes waiting, ladies."

"Can't dance with a potato, Kenny!" one of the women called back.

Everyone laughed, even Rett as she shut her locker door and made sure her apron strings weren't dangling. The ladies were in a good mood that Friday morning. They reminded her of the women she'd been surrounded by while growing up. Hardworking, decent women who had one another's backs through thick and thin, helping with kids and chores as they could.

"Well, then, you can dance with my carrot, Tilda," Thorpe retorted.

That got most of the women cackling.

"More like a green bean," someone said. Laughter became hoots.

"I heard that," came Thorpe's voice, though he didn't sound mad. "Let's move it."

The same prompt to get to work sounded from across the hall as Thorpe yelled to the men. Rett didn't hear any amusing rejoinders from that side. Maybe the women were more apt to tease Thorpe.

"How's the first few days been, Loretta?"

Rett smiled shyly at Lana, one of the younger women who worked the chopping table behind Rett's. Playing the quiet newcomer often allowed her to go unnoticed as the women talked among themselves. Topics ranged from family to the latest on the *Titanic* tragedy, but little about B&H. "So far, so good. Though my hands are a little achy."

They followed the stream of women through the locker room to the door. The space was clean and smelled of perfumes of various kinds, as well as a slight antiseptic sharpness from cleaners and the soap at the sinks near the toilets. Rett was sure the cheery blue paint on the walls and colorful doors were by design. Margot seemed like the sort to make even a room like this pleasant for her employees.

"Yeah, it can be rough at first." Lana flexed her raised hand. "You'll get stronger. I use Sumner's Liniment before work and before bedtime." She held her hand closer to Rett's face. "Smells good too."

It smelled like mothballs to Rett, but she smiled and nodded. "I'll be sure to pick some up."

In the four days since starting her job at B&H, Rett had found the employees generally happy with the company and Margot—though they could always be holding things back from the new girl. But she could also see why they would be content. Sure, it was constant physical work—her back and shoulder had been crying for three days—but breaks were offered twice a shift, everyone got half an hour for lunch or supper, and the pay was comparable to similar jobs. B&H even had a program in place for advancement on salaries or low-interest loans for every employee.

It all sounded too good to be true, which told Rett something *could* be going on. Keep employees happy and they'll pretend they don't see violations or shortcuts being taken. She hoped she was wrong. The B&H employees didn't deserve to suffer for someone else's misdeeds. But that seemed to be the way, didn't it? The folks on the lower rungs took the brunt of most corporate fallout.

Rett and the rest of the women greeted the men from their room across the hall and lined up to punch the time clock before passing through the double doors into the vast prep room. Thorpe stood off to the side, leaning down to speak to another man so they could be heard over the conveyor belt motors warming up. Choppers checked their knives and put their sharpening steels to use as baskets were filled with whole vegetables at one end by boys and young men pushing carts. Baskets with smaller mesh openings at the other end of tables contained the diced vegetables before they were hauled to the canner.

Uniformity in size was critical to efficiency and even cooking, and it had taken Rett a little time to get the knack of it. Thankfully, spring potatoes were similar in size, and the carrots required no more than a few chops. She wasn't sure she'd ever be as fast as some of the women at the tables, though. There were a few times they stood idle, waiting for a fresh basket of vegetables while Rett's was still half full.

The clatter and chatter of the chopping section filled her ears as she considered how best to explore more of the B&H grounds she had memorized from Margot's blueprints. Her ten-minute breaks weren't enough to get much done, but the half hour for lunch was useful. While the others gathered outside to eat and smoke, or in the staff dining room where they could sit for a while if the weather wasn't agreeable, Rett walked the grounds to familiarize herself. Not everyone took lunch at the same time, and certain buildings seemed to have no one entering or leaving.

Within a few days, she felt she was getting a feel for the place. But she was running out of time. The twenty-fifth had passed without any sort of blowup, but the person receiving the payments wouldn't stay quiet for long. They'd either find another way to get their money or expose . . . something about B&H. She couldn't let that happen. Not on her first case, and not to someone like Margot.

The morning went by fast enough, and when it was time for the section lunch break, Rett quickly wiped her hands on her apron and headed to the doors leading outside. Some of the others followed but stayed close to the benches near the wall to eat, smoke, and socialize. Rett half ran toward the corner of the building so Lana wouldn't call out to her. Nice girl, but there was a job to do.

On the back side of the building, Rett slowed to a walk. It was a warm spring day, with a breeze coming from the north that felt refreshing after the steamy environs of the cannery. The other buildings were connected to the main cannery via brick walkways. The reinforced paths made it easier to roll carts to and from locations without traveling the narrow roads used to access buildings with vehicles.

Rett had already checked out the nearby vegetable stores and label production buildings. Her goal today was the farther afield and noisier can manufacturing building, where a smokestack spewed sooty fumes and the clatter and hum of metal and machines could be heard from one hundred feet away.

Cognizant of the time, she hurried around the side of the metalworks building, avoiding the delivery bay where a flatbed truck was being unloaded. A quick glance in that direction showed a brown-haired man in work clothes standing with his back to her, hands on his hips, watching others unload the truck while he smoked a cigarette. The driver, she figured. A sign on the side panel of the truck read MARTIN SCRAP & METAL FABRICATION.

She ducked around the corner to find an unlocked door and slipped inside. Hot metal, sweat, and heat rode the banging and clanging and hissing coming from the works room. Sparks flared where cutters and welders created the containers and lids for B&H. Margot had said it was more price-effective to make their own at times, that it had initially cost the company to do so but was well worth it. By the looks of the specialized machines filling the space, Rett could only imagine what that cost added up to.

Staying in the shadows as best she could, Rett skirted the outer wall of the noisy manufacturing facility. The workers were mostly men from what she could tell, with women here and there. All wore coveralls, goggles, and leather gloves. There was little to no conversation other than the occasional shout to a nearby coworker over running machinery and clanging metal.

She watched the workers cutting the sheets of tin-plated steel to size, the next workers putting them through rollers to solder the side seams, then others crimping the bottoms. The empty cans were crated, eventually to be cleaned, filled, capped, processed, and labeled elsewhere. The purpose of the building was making cans. Nothing more and nothing less.

What felt like a ham came down on Rett's shoulder. She jumped and yelped at the same time, turning with her fist clenched and cocked. Heart racing, she stared up at the goggled man before her. His faded blue coveralls were wrinkled and a bit grubby. Sweat beaded across his brown forehead. He whipped off the goggles with one ungloved hand, leaving ring impressions around his hard brown eyes.

"Whadaya doin' in here?" He yelled to be heard over the machines, though Rett heard the irritation in his voice clear as day. "You can't be wanderin' around."

"Sorry," she yelled back. "I was just curious."

The man rolled his eyes and gestured for her to follow him.

Heart still thudding, she did. He led her to the door where she'd entered. Closing it behind them, they were able to converse in mostly normal levels.

"Ya can't just walk in there, miss." He wiped the sweat

off his forehead with his forearm. "People get hurt if they ain't where they're supposed to be."

Rett wondered if that was a threat or an observation regarding the job.

"What's yer name?"

She hesitated. She wasn't particularly concerned about being fired, but should act it. "L-Loretta March. I-I just started." Putting on the most innocent and pleading face she could, Rett grabbed his sleeve. "Please don't tell Mr. Thorpe. My ma will kill me if I get canned. I just wanna see what goes on over here, is all."

His lips pressed together, the man heaved a sigh. "Okay, okay. Just don't go wandering places, ya hear? If ya wanna see how things work, ask. One of us can give ya the nickel tour."

Genuinely relieved that she hadn't gotten in too much trouble, Rett gave him a bright smile. "Gee, thanks, that'd be swell, um . . . ?"

Giving her a more appreciative look, he grinned and held out his right hand. "Vinny. Nice to meet ya."

"Nice to meet you too." She shook his hand quickly. "I'd better get back. Thanks, Vinny. See ya 'round."

Rett hurried back around to the front side of the building, hoping she wouldn't have to figure out a way to avoid Vinny again. As she rounded the corner, the truck in the delivery bay started up, belching a cloud of black smoke. The driver waved out the window to the B&H workers before putting the vehicle into gear. He drove past Rett, giving her a wink and a nod, a cigarette dangling between his thin lips, before concentrating on the road.

Rett's heart stumbled, then raced once again. "Holy Hannah."

The driver was the man Margot had clobbered at Mrs. Gilroy's house.

Fourteen

Margot arrived at B&H just as the first lunch shift returned to work and the second streamed out to enjoy the spring day. She greeted the longtime employees she had known since she was a girl, asked about families and health. Climbing the stairs to the second-floor offices, Margot turned to look down across the floor in time to see Rett returning to her chopping table. They made eye contact. Rett gave a subtle nod, the intensity of her stare speaking volumes.

Had she found something?

Margot's mouth went dry. She nodded back, then focused on the door at the top of the stairs. She'd arrange for Bascom to pick Rett up and bring her to the house this evening.

Once in the glassed-in hallway, she shut the door behind her and took a breath to calm herself. What could Rett have found? How bad was it going to be? Part of her didn't want to know, but that was why she'd hired the investigator—to learn things she didn't want to know.

Muffled yet elevated voices behind Hiram's closed door pulled Margot out of her thoughts. What was going on in there? She wouldn't interfere, but she'd be sure to ask Hiram about it later.

Calm and collected once again, Margot headed to Julia Blumfeld's office. Though the door was ajar, she knocked a few times before opening it. Inside, Julia was at her desk eating a sandwich, taking care to avoid dropping any fillings on her pristine white blouse. She waved Margot in, tucking a loose strand of black hair behind her ear with her free hand.

"I don't mean to interrupt your lunch, Julia. I can come back."

The accountant took a drink from her water glass, then wiped her lips with a napkin. "Not to worry, Margot. Please, come in."

Margot entered the office, closing the door behind her. Julia glanced at her calendar. It wasn't unusual for Margot to have private meetings with her, but they were typically arranged in advance.

As she took the seat across from Julia's desk, Margot noticed she wasn't sitting in her regular chair. In fact, it was nowhere to be seen. Her chest tightened, remembering Mrs. Gilroy. She couldn't blame Julia for getting it out of her office and made a mental note to order a new chair for the accountant.

"How are you doing, Julia?"

Julia wrapped the rest of her sandwich in its wax paper cover and set it aside. "All right. Still a little in shock. How are you?"

Worried about the company. Angry at Randolph. Guilty about losing touch with Mrs. Gilroy. Margot smiled sadly. "I'm well."

The other woman nodded, and Margot noticed she'd gained a few more lines and gray hairs since last they'd met. She supposed they all had in recent days.

Julia looked at her expectantly. She wouldn't come out and ask Margot why she was there, but curiosity showed in her expression.

"How well did you know Mrs. Gilroy?" she asked.

Julia stared at her for a moment or two. "We weren't personal friends, but got on all right here at the office."

"When was the last time you spoke to her or saw her?"

Her expression turned sour. "That police person asked me the same thing the other day. We hadn't spoken or seen each other since just after Mr. Harriman passed."

Lieutenant Presley had returned? Since the coroner had determined Mrs. Gilroy had a natural death, there was little reason to investigate. Had something changed? Had the coroner learned otherwise? Did Presley know more?

The thought left her feeling sick. How much time did she really have to investigate before Presley questioned her again about whatever brought him back? And what would it look like to have a policeman sniffing about when employees were present? Word would surely get out then, alerting the papers to something being amiss. Would whoever received those payments think it was her fault and jeopardize B&H?

"Did you tell the lieutenant anything he found interesting or important?" Margot tried to keep her voice casual.

Julia shrugged. "I doubt it. He asked why she might have come here, but I had no idea. Nostalgia, perhaps?"

That was what it appeared to be, but the note Mrs. Gilroy had been writing suggested something more. Only Julia and the police didn't know about that, did they?

"What did you and Mrs. Gilroy talk about last time you saw her?"

Julia gave her a curious look. Was Margot going too far?

"Just cleaning up some paperwork. I contacted her about a medical claim she'd signed off on months before." Julia shrugged. "I only remember because we chatted a few minutes about how her retirement was going after she clarified some information. She planned to do some traveling in Europe and I told her where I'd visited."

"Why had *she* signed off on the claim?" That hadn't been part of Mrs. Gilroy's job description.

"It had come through while I was gone, helping my sister after her baby was born. Mrs. Gilroy brought it to Hiram for approval, but there were some details missing. It had been misfiled, and luckily I'd found it quite by accident. I called Mrs. Gilroy and obtained the corrections." She shrugged. "Nothing out of the ordinary."

Perhaps not, but Julia didn't have several lists of questionable entries that looked like payments.

"What were the circumstances of the claim?"

As safe as they tried to be at all B&H facilities, accidents happened, and injuries were to be expected. Thankfully, as far as she knew no one had been seriously hurt, though Mrs. Gilroy's note said otherwise. Did that have to do with these claims?

"A bakery worker in the Yonkers plant, I believe." Julia rose and went over to her wall of filing cabinets. She pulled one open and began searching the folder tabs. "Someone named Binney? Bonney? It was a reimbursement, not a payment to the hospital. Sorry, I can't recall all the details."

Margot smiled. "I'd be more than impressed if you could, considering all the names and numbers that cross your desk in a given week."

Julia chuckled but kept looking through the drawer. She closed that one and opened another. "That's strange."

Margot's good cheer dropped. "What is?"

"I can't find the file." She searched a second drawer but to no avail. Closing that one, she stood with her fists on her hips, her back still to Margot. "Where did I—Oh!" Julia turned to a different set of drawers and pulled one open. After a few moments, she slid a folder out. "Here we are. It was Bonney, in the former employee claims drawer."

She handed the folder to Margot. The tab read BONNEY, A. J.—MEDICAL.

Margot opened the folder. "*Former* employee?"

"Apparently." Julia returned to her chair. "He paid the hospital and sent us the receipt for services so we could reimburse him. Mrs. Gilroy said he had left the bakery, though."

"How did she know?" Margot opened the folder, noting there were only a few pages, one of which looked like a hospital receipt of services for fifteen dollars.

Julia shrugged, giving Margot a look again. "I assumed she knew someone up there or had been told at some point and just forgot to let me know."

That did sound reasonable, and Margot knew now she'd pressed too far. But she also knew Mrs. Gilroy had come to Julia's office for a reason. Was this file it? Were there more?

"I'm sure that's what it was." Margot stood. "I'll get this back to you soon. Thank you, Julia."

Julia rose. "Margot, what's going on?"

She didn't think the accountant was involved in whatever Mrs. Gilroy had alluded to in her note, but Margot couldn't be sure. She wasn't sure of much lately.

"I'm just looking at a few things. I promise to let you know details if necessary." She held the folder up. "Thanks. We'll talk soon."

One advantage of being the head of the company was not needing to explain herself, except to the shareholders, and she did as little of that as she could get away with. She didn't like leaving Julia in the dark, but for now it was for the best.

Margot entered the hallway, shutting Julia's door behind her in time to hear the stairway door close and see a man heading down. She went to the window. The man from Hiram's office with whom he'd been having words? He was of average height, in a gray suit, carrying his hat and overcoat. His hair was thinning on top. She watched him until he disappeared.

Who was he?

She strode to Hiram's door and knocked. Hiram answered quickly, as if he was standing right behind the door.

"Hello, Margot. I'm just headed out." Sure enough, his overcoat was on and his hat was in his hand. "What can I do for you?"

"Who were you were talking to?" She gestured toward the door. "I saw him leave but can't place him."

Hiram blinked at her a couple of times. "That was Charlie

Meade." The name sounded vaguely familiar, but Margot still couldn't place him. When Hiram realized this, he added, "From the state food inspector's office."

That was it. She'd met him briefly at some meeting or another several years ago.

"Of course. What did he want?" If there was trouble with the state, she needed to know, especially now.

"Just a change in the schedule," Hiram said, brushing off the question. "This recent spate of food-borne illnesses that has been in the papers is making everyone jumpy. The state inspectors want to show they're on top of it."

The state trying to get ahead of things? What a pleasant surprise.

"Those newspaper reports have been concerning. But he came all the way out for that? A letter would have sufficed." Something wasn't right. State workers weren't known for personal visits. Particularly ones with raised voices.

"He was on his way past and decided to stop in." Hiram retreated into his private office and grabbed an envelope off his desk. He handed it to her. "Nothing important."

Not that she didn't trust what he said, but Margot removed the letter and read it. Sure enough, though they had just been through their inspection before the new year, B&H facilities were now rescheduled for spring. She put the letter in the envelope and handed it back, still uneasy.

"That's fine. We have nothing to hide." She hoped. She searched Hiram's expression as she said it.

Hiram smiled, but he appeared stressed. The lines near his mouth and eyes seemed deeper. "Anything else? I have a meeting with that new advertising company you were interested in."

Margot stepped back into the hall as Hiram put the letter back on his desk. He locked his door and donned his hat.

"I'll give you the gist of the meeting Monday, yes?" He offered a small smile at her questioning look. "I'm headed to Philadelphia later this evening. My nephew's wedding is tomorrow."

"Of course. Give them all my best."

Hiram quick-walked to the door leading down to the cannery floor, closing it firmly behind himself.

She watched him follow the same path Charlie Meade had taken. Something had been bothering Hiram, and Margot was pretty damn sure it wasn't that he was late for a meeting.

Fifteen

Later that afternoon, Margot almost felt guilty about going to the Division of Food Safety and Inspection office without telling Hiram or Julia or anyone else. Almost. But damnation, this was her company at risk. Her name. It was difficult enough to consider her father and Mrs. Gilroy involved in some sort of illegal or nefarious activities—now she had to include Hiram, even Julia?

A headache throbbed behind her right eye as Margot climbed the stairs to the fourth-floor offices. There was an elevator, but she was determined to be more physically active, plus she needed to vent some frustration. She felt like hitting something. Didn't women box? Surely they did. Rett would know.

Margot entered the fourth-floor hall. Typical of government buildings, it wasn't particularly inspiring décor, but handsomely paneled. A dozen offices, six on each side, ran the length of the building. She stopped at the one with Meade's name painted on it, knocked, and went in without waiting for an invitation.

"Yes?" Meade sat at a plain desk, coat off, an array of papers in front of him. Round spectacles reflected the overhead light. Recognition dawned in his eyes and he rose, reaching for his suit coat draped over the chair back at the same time. "Miss Harriman. What a surprise."

He shrugged into the coat and came around to the front of the desk, a friendly but bemused smile on his face. They shook hands and he offered her a seat.

"What can I do for you?" he asked when he was sitting behind his desk once again.

Margot got as comfortable as she could on the hard, ladder-back chair. She smiled politely at Meade. "I saw you had been meeting with Hiram Potter earlier. Sorry I missed you, though Hiram filled me in."

A slight lie, but Meade didn't need to know that.

His eyes widened behind his spectacles. "Oh? I hadn't expected him to do that. I mean, considering . . ."

She narrowed her gaze at him. "B&H is my company, Mr. Meade. Anything and everything that happens to it, in it, or by it, is mine to know."

Meade rested his forearms on the desk, fingertips tapping together. "Of course, of course. Glad to hear. So you're . . . amenable to the situation?"

She chose her words carefully. "Amenable? Do I have a say in the matter?"

Inspections weren't negotiable, they just were. What was *he* referring to?

He chuckled. "Amenable isn't quite the correct word, I suppose. Understanding, perhaps. You have nothing to worry about as long as our agreement holds." Meade leaned forward slightly and lowered his voice. "So, do you have it with you?"

She stared at him, unsure of what the man was after. "Do I have what with me?"

The inspector laughed with a hint of nervousness. "You said you spoke to Potter. I assume he gave you the details to maintain the arrangement."

It took every ounce of control for Margot to keep a tight rein on the flurry of emotions cascading through her. Anger. Indignation. Confusion. Frustration. All relegated to biting her tongue and clenching her fists. To help remain outwardly calm, she looked away from Meade's self-satisfied smile, focusing on the framed certificates and diplomas hung on the wall behind him. A commendation from the Yonkers Chamber of Commerce. A diploma from Yonkers College.

The realization of what Meade alluded to made her hands shake; she gripped her handbag like it was a lifeline. He was somewhere in the little blue book or on the neatly scribed pages Rett found in the safety-deposit box, she was sure of it now. He was who the payments were being sent to. Was he the only one? What would happen if she didn't pay? Headlines shouting SCANDAL! in the *Times* and the *Tribune* spun through her head. She'd said she knew what was going on, that she was involved. He had her.

You fool, she admonished herself.

Margot inhaled deeply, slowly letting the breath out until her chest didn't quiver. "The arrangement. Yes. Hiram told me, but I thought you and I could chat."

Meade sighed, his smile turned patronizing. It was a look Margot had seen all too often across desks and conference tables when she'd sat beside Randolph, asking valid questions or making solid points. That certain men felt so very *amused* by her presence would never cease to irritate.

"Miss Harriman, there is little to 'chat' about. Either agree to the arrangement, or . . ."

He let the sentence trail off, shrugging with his hands palm up, as if whatever happened next would be out of his control. Margot knew that was far from the truth.

Her jaws tight, she silently counted to ten before saying, "Remind me how much."

"One hundred." He paused, the delight shining in his eyes. "A month."

"One hundred a month?" The words came out louder

than either of them expected, judging from Meade's wide-eyed reaction.

"Please, keep your voice down, Miss Harriman. Neither of us will gain from having to explain ourselves." He smoothed his hair back. "Now, do you have it? April's installment is past due."

And if Margot didn't pay, Meade would reveal some terrible thing he'd been keeping over B&H. There was no way out of it, at least not in the short term, but she was damned sure not "amenable" to being blackmailed.

Unable to stand being in his presence a moment longer, Margot rose. "You'll get it."

"By Monday, if you please, Miss Harriman."

She strode to the door and yanked it open. Half turned back to him, she dismissed a dozen epithets before settling on something safer. "You are a wretched little man, Mr. Meade."

He replied, but Margot was in the hall, slamming the door behind her, and didn't hear him.

The man and woman coming down the hall, however, surely had heard her. They passed her, curious. Margot simply stared at them until they turned down another hall.

"Son of a bitch," she muttered, stomping her way to the stairwell.

Sixteen

Rett had been to the Harriman house twice before, but she was again impressed when Bascom swung around the circular driveway and parked at the front entrance. Despite its size and Randolph Harriman's desire to show off, it was truly a lovely home, not some pretentious showpiece. Rich, but understated and real. Much like Margot Baxter Harriman herself.

Bascom opened the front passenger door for her—Rett couldn't see why she should ride in the back, especially when they had great conversations about the Dodgers and the Giants.

"Miss Harriman said she'd be in her office," he said.

Rett stepped into the foyer and unbuttoned her coat. "Thanks for the lift."

"My pleasure, though I think you're wrong about the Giants. They're going all the way again." He grinned when she gave a good-natured scoff. "Ring when you're done and I'll see you home."

"Thanks, Mr. Bascom."

He sketched a quick bow and left.

Rett knocked on the solid oak door, which was not closed all the way, so Margot's invitation to come in was clear enough. Rett pushed the door open and started to greet the other woman but was brought up short when she saw the state of the room.

Papers and folders were piled on chairs, the sideboard, the desk, any horizontal surface. The drawers of the filing cabinet were open with more papers and files half pulled out. Margot stood at the desk, hair disheveled, a streak of grime across her cheek, clutching a crystal tumbler.

"What the hell happened?" Rett asked. "Were you robbed?"

The usually cool and collected heiress and company president looked up. The muscles of her jaws worked as if she was chewing nails. The absolute rage in her dark eyes, coupled with the nearly empty decanter on the desk, told Rett there was a lot more going on than mere theft.

"Shut the door," Margot commanded, then seemed to catch herself. She took a calming breath. "Please."

Rett did as she was asked. "What's going on?"

"I got this from Julia Blumfeld today," she said, picking up a file folder off the desk and holding it out to Rett. "And this afternoon, now knowing more or less what to look for, I found others like them down in the basement."

Rett took the folder and looked through the few pages within. A medical compensation claim for one A. J. Bonney who was injured while on the job at B&H's bakery in Yonkers. Some sort of accident last year that Bonney had paid for out of pocket and was reimbursed by the company. Signed off by Giana Gilroy and Hiram Potter.

"What am I supposed to be seeing here? These look legit."

"Exactly," Margot said. "Except A. J. Bonney doesn't exist. Sorry. I don't know that for sure. What I *do* know is that A. J. Bonney never worked for B&H."

Rett glanced through the file again. "According to this, he—are they a 'he'?—started in May of 1910 and got hurt August of 1911."

"I've been through every employment record we have here and there is nothing on them but that file."

Rett wasn't one to jump to conclusions, but the situation certainly put her suspicious nature on alert. "Paperwork can get lost. Or maybe it's stuck in a box somewhere in the Yonkers office."

Margot poured more whisky into her glass and drank it down. She picked up a small pile of folders. "Maybe, but here are five more ghost employees who got hurt and were paid back over the last few years. I can't find anything on them either. There could be more."

Suspicion jumped from alerted to alarmed. "Holy Hannah. How did no one spot this sooner?"

"Files and records can be hidden during audits. If the payouts were in cash, then it can be easier." She spoke with a matter-of-fact attitude that implied she'd had all too much time to consider how this could have happened and, perhaps, who was responsible.

"And cash doesn't require a second signature if you don't go through a bank," Rett said, hazarding a guess that most larger businesses ran that way. Margot nodded. "That two thousand dollars in the secret safety-deposit box makes sense now. The money didn't go to these ghost employees, so where was it supposed to go?"

Margot's eyes hardened. "At least a good portion of it to Charlie Meade."

"Who's Charlie Meade?"

Margot told her about meeting with the state food inspector after seeing him leave Hiram Potter's office earlier in the day. She'd had her suspicions going in, and came out not only assured of Meade's blackmail scheme but involved in it.

"Hiram knows the details," Rett said. She had never met the man, but Margot had spoken highly of him, and told her how close he was to her and the Harriman family. That sort of betrayal couldn't be sitting well.

"He does. I'll get in touch with him tomorrow." Something bothersome crossed Margot's face. "Damn it. He's gone for the weekend. I won't be able to talk to him until Monday."

It was only Friday evening. More than two long days for Margot to stew.

"Meade wants his money by then," Margot continued. She sat down on her chair and sighed, looking over the stacks of papers, then up at Rett. "I almost forgot. This afternoon at the cannery, you seemed to have something to tell me."

With all the shocking information Margot had laid out, Rett had also nearly forgotten why she'd been brought to the house tonight.

"Right. When I was looking around the grounds, I spotted the man you nearly brained at Mrs. Gilroy's."

Margot's cheeks pinkened. "I've never hit anyone like that and hope to never do so again. But you saw him at the cannery? An employee?"

She sounded horrified by the idea, and Rett was happy to relieve her of that burden, at least.

"No, a driver for a company out of Yonkers. Martin Scrap and Metal Fabrication."

"They supply our can materials. Are you sure it was the same man? It was hard to see well at Mrs. Gilroy's."

Rett nodded. "I got a good look at him when I checked to make sure he was alive. Whoever had him go over to Mrs. Gilroy's that night knows exactly what's going on."

Which could be anyone from Hiram Potter to Julia Blumfeld to someone on the canning line.

Margot scrubbed her palms up and down her face, smearing the grime. She rubbed at the dirt on her hands. "What is happening at my company, Rett? Blackmail. Break-ins. I don't know who to trust anymore."

Her heart went out to the other woman. To have your world crumbling around you with no idea which direction the hits were coming from had to be beyond difficult.

"We have some good leads," Rett said with assurance. "I'll check out this Meade guy. Give me what you can on him. A friend in the city records office often goes in on Saturdays or Sundays to work on his novel. I might be able to find something. You can't talk to Potter until Monday, but once you have more information, we can figure out how to get you out of Meade's 'arrangement.' In the meantime . . ." She got to her feet. "Let's get you out of here."

Margot stared up at her for a moment. "You want to go out?"

"Yep. Shiloh's on at nine with the Great Todd. Afterward, there will be an opening night party. CeeCee and I are going. Come with us. It'll do you good."

Rett wasn't one to mix business and personal time, but at this moment, Margot Baxter Harriman needed a friend, and she needed to forget her troubles for at least a little while.

"I don't think so, Rett." She looked down at her smudged blouse. "I'm a mess, the office is a mess . . ."

Her world was a mess, was what she wasn't saying. But whose wasn't?

Rett shook her head. "Dirt washes off and these papers will be here tomorrow. Come on, Margot. A few hours away from this won't hurt. It will do you a hell of a lot of good, actually. When's the last time you let yourself have some fun for fun's sake?"

By the wince that furrowed Margot's brow, Rett would bet it had been too long.

She thought she would have dig up some more arguments to persuade Margot, but to Rett's surprise, the other woman stood. "All right. A few hours."

Seventeen

Margot couldn't remember the last time she'd gone out just for fun. No board members to wine and dine. No suppliers or bankers to impress. Just enjoying herself and the friends she was with.

Yes, friends. She, Rett, and CeeCee had chatted and kept one another in stitches from the time they'd left Rett and CeeCee's apartment all the way to the theater. Bit by bit, the stress of the day fell away with each laugh. She hadn't felt this close to anyone since her college days.

She rarely let herself relax, even with people she truly liked. Upon graduation, she'd had to become the business-minded heiress, the serious woman in whom the B&H shareholders could find no fault. Frivolity had no place in their world, and so no place in hers. But damn it, she missed the simple joy of doing something for the sake of fun and fun alone.

Now, sitting with Rett and CeeCee among the rapt audience, cigar and cigarette smoke tingeing the air blue and itching her nose, she watched the final trick of the night. The orchestra played a peppy tune while Shiloh, in a scandalous sparkly blue leotard and matching heels, pulled a shimmering silver curtain hung on a circular, wheeled frame from the rear of the stage. For his part, the Great Todd was suspended upside down and bound with padlocked chains over the stage. Shiloh positioned the framed curtain around Todd, completely enclosing him, then secured the gap with another chain and lock.

Grasping the frame, she walked steadily in a circle around Todd at center stage, long legs taking her into the deep shadows at the rear of the stage as wolf whistles sounded from the audience.

The framed curtain continued to move uninterrupted, concealing the magician. The end Shiloh had been holding came into view, now being pulled by the Great Todd himself.

The audience gasped and cheered. The magician withdrew a key from his pocket and opened the lock that secured the frame. He pushed on the frame, opening the curtain to reveal Shiloh, in chains and hanging upside down in the middle of the stage.

Wild applause shook the theater.

Rett, CeeCee, and Margot jumped to their feet with the rest of the appreciative audience. Margot's cheeks ached from smiling. "Brilliant!"

Stage assistants lowered Shiloh and unlocked her bonds, helping her gracefully gain her feet. She and the Great Todd clasped hands and bowed several times.

"How did they do that?" CeeCee asked, yelling over the noise of the crowd.

Rett merely shrugged.

The orchestra—eight musicians and the conductor—increased the tempo of the piece as Shiloh and the Great Todd strode off the stage.

The master of ceremonies came on with his megaphone, gesturing to the departing act. "The Great Todd and his lovely assistant Shiloh, ladies and gentlemen!" He waited for the hoots and clapping to subside a little, then continued. "Be sure to come back for more songs, dance, laughs, and mesmerizing entertainment here at the Barsky Theater! Good night!"

The orchestra resumed their frenetic playing, violin bows sawing back and forth, the trumpet and trombone glinting in the overhead lights as they swung in tempo.

"That was amazing." Margot spoke loud enough to be heard over the orchestra, something she'd never do at the Metropolitan Opera House, and followed CeeCee and Rett. The three of them filed out of the row and into the aisle, joining the other couple of hundred attendees working their way toward the doors.

"Shiloh and Todd put on a fun show," Rett said. "Come on. We'll meet Shiloh over at the stage door."

Rett led the way through the small lobby, holding CeeCee's hand. CeeCee reached back for Margot. Smiling at each other, they clasped hands. They allowed the current of the chatting crowd to pull them outside into the cool spring night. When there was room, Rett guided the three of them away from the throng. Head buzzing with residual sound, Margot let go of CeeCee, but she noticed Rett still held on to CeeCee's other hand.

"This way," Rett said. They headed around to the side of the building, down a relatively clean and lit alley.

Several admirers were already there waiting at the base of a set of metal stairs that led up to a door. Margot heard them speak the names of a couple of the other acts, singers, and comedians. None mentioned Shiloh or the Great Todd. Pity. They were the best on stage that night, though Margot admitted to herself that her opinion might be a little skewed toward the blonde being an acquaintance and all.

Not long after the admirers at the door had their opportunity to greet their favorites and disperse, Shiloh Wallace came out. She wore an outfit similar to the trousers, waistcoat, and overcoat Margot had met her in the previous week, though this ensemble had a finer cut. It looked quite good on her. Dressing that way was against the "anti-masquerade" law of New York, but Shiloh didn't seem concerned about breaking it. She strode down the stairs with a confident swagger. When she caught Margot's gaze, her smile grew.

Margot smiled back, attributing the flutter in her belly to the excitement and joy of the evening.

"Brava!" Rett proclaimed, smiling and applauding. Margot and CeeCee followed suit.

Once again, the friendship Margot felt between them sent a comforting warmth through her. When had she lost that sense of closeness with other women? With . . . anyone?

Shiloh bowed at the waist. "Thank you, thank you. Glad you enjoyed it."

"It was thrilling," Margot said. Shiloh's gaze locked on hers again, and Margot felt something else stir deep in her belly.

The blonde offered a playful grin that Margot couldn't help but return. "I'm all about the thrills." She glanced at Rett and CeeCee. "Ready for a bit of refreshment and fun? The party's at Dumphrey's."

"Oh, they make a delish Gibson," CeeCee said with glee.

"You just like gin," Rett teased as they started down the street.

"This is true," CeeCee replied.

Rett and CeeCee led the way while Margot and Shiloh strolled behind them. West Brooklyn at midnight should have been quiet, but it was Friday and several small vaudeville venues had just let out. Margot and Shiloh chatted about the show and show business on the short walk to the saloon.

Inside Dumphrey's, the smell of smoke, beer, and perfume hung in the air. The conversations and laughter were loud yet inviting. The jovial atmosphere was a far cry from the staid dinners Margot usually attended, where even the supposed "parties" were more sedate. The saloon crowd wasn't wild or out of control, just obviously enjoying themselves.

Shiloh ushered them to a corner table where they could all sit and hear one another, mostly. Catching Margot's eye, she wiggled her fingers and reached toward Margot's left ear. Margot smiled and held still, recalling the Great Todd's very same motion as he was about to enact some magic trick. Shiloh brought her hand back in front of Margot, a shiny coin flipping between her fingers.

"First round's on me," she said with a wink and headed toward the bar.

Margot took in the crowd of men and women, some of whom were still in costume from whatever show they'd been in, appreciating their sense of freedom. They moved among one another's groups as if everyone knew everyone else, hands on backs or shoulders, hugs between men and women, or two men, or two women without a care as to who saw what.

She brought her attention back to her companions. Rett and CeeCee sat closer together than even the small table required. Margot couldn't help grinning. "So tell me how you two became friends. Rett told me she met Shiloh at school."

CeeCee and Rett exchanged looks and broke into laughter.

"You tell her," CeeCee said. "I take no responsibility."

Rett shook her head, smiling. "Denying it won't make it less true, Cee." She turned to Margot. "I was questioning a witness—"

"Who was on my hospital ward. In traction, no less," CeeCee interrupted.

"Easier to keep him in one place." Rett shrugged, and Margot laughed despite the image in her head. "I was questioning him, but before I could get an answer—"

"It was well past visiting hours."

Rett gave CeeCee a sidelong look. "Do you want to tell it?"

CeeCee waved her off. "No, no. Carry on."

Margot's cheeks ached from smiling.

"Anyway, before I could get an answer from the guy, CeeCee came in on her rounds and threw me out. I explained he had ducked out on his wife and three kids and I was trying to get them some sort of financial support."

Margot's jaw dropped. "How terrible. Did you get that for them?"

CeeCee rolled her eyes. "He was no deadbeat. Not married and no kids. That was the story she told so I'd let her back in the following evening."

Rett shrugged off the fib. "He was the lookout for a burglary ring, and when I came back the next day, CeeCee told me about others who'd been visiting him. I sweet-talked her into letting me return to see them for myself, and then got the guy to name names."

Margot glanced between the two of them. "You solved the case together."

The two women's gazes held for a moment and they smiled.

"And a beautiful friendship was born," CeeCee said.

If Margot was any sort of judge of body language, it was more than friendship.

Shiloh returned then with a tray holding two tall glasses of beer and two stemmed glasses with clear liquid and a pearl onion each.

"Wasn't sure what you wanted," she said to Margot as she set a beer in front of Rett and one of the Gibsons before CeeCee. "So pick, and I'll take the other."

"Is the beer any good?" she asked. It had been a while since she'd had a beer.

"Made from the best water they can get from the bottom of the Hudson," Rett said.

Margot made a face and Shiloh laughed as she slid the Gibson in front of her. "Take this one. I'm used to the brew here."

"To a great show," Rett said, holding up her glass.

They toasted and drank. CeeCee was right. Gin wasn't Margot's go-to liquor, but the Gibson was rather tasty.

"How did you get into show business?" Margot asked Shiloh between sips.

The blonde wiped the foam of her beer off her upper lip. Her other hand dipped into her coat pocket. "A hobby that became something more."

"Oh, here we go." Rett grinned.

Shiloh started shuffling the deck of cards she retrieved. "My grandfather taught me and my brother how to do card tricks. Good for the mind and the dexterity, he'd said."

Dexterity for lock and pocket picking, Margot supposed. Her own grandfather had taught her how to balance a checkbook.

Shiloh fanned out the cards face up to show they were all mixed together, then set them into a neat stack once again. Margot smiled as she was handed the deck.

"Hold them under the table and make sure there are fifty-two cards," Shiloh said. "Fan them out and pick one. Don't show anyone. Touch it with your finger, then close the deck."

Shiloh purposely turned her head away. Margot did as she was asked, choosing the queen of spades. She straightened the cards in the deck and brought them above the table. "Done."

Shiloh turned around. She took the cards, her fingertips gently stroking Margot's palm. A fission of electricity seemed to travel up her arm as she stared at the magician's assistant. Still holding each other's gazes, as if no one else was in the room, Shiloh shuffled the deck then set it on the table.

"Cut the deck and choose a half," she said.

Margot picked up half the deck from the pile and set it beside the other half. After a moment's thought, she tapped the top of the other half. Shiloh took up that half, held it to her ear, and flicked the edges with her thumb, blue eyes narrowed, as if listening.

"Nope," she said, and set the half deck down. She picked up the second half and "listened" again. "Not here either." She put the deck together and slid it over to Margot. "Go ahead and count them. Face down, if you would."

Margot picked up the deck without looking at the cards and counted them onto the table. ". . . Forty-eight, forty-nine, fifty, fifty-one," she said as she laid the last card on top of the deck. She gazed up at Shiloh, eyebrows raised in question.

As she had with the coin trick at the start of the evening, Shiloh wagged her fingers and reached toward Margot's left ear. This time, however, Margot felt the other woman brush her earlobe, sending a shiver through her. Shiloh pulled her hand back, the queen of spades between her fingers. Grinning, she held it out to Margot.

Rett and CeeCee looked at her, anticipation brightening their eyes, and when Margot nodded, they clapped enthusiastically. "Brava!"

Margot plucked the card from Shiloh's hand. There were no marks or imperfections or anything on the card she could see that would have stood out to the magician's assistant. "How?"

Shiloh took the card back. "Can't reveal my secrets now, can I?" She had the queen join the others and shuffled. With another flourish, the deck disappeared. "Another round of drinks?"

For the next hour, and a third round on Margot, she felt quite at ease with the women at the table. They talked about all manner of things, from the show to women's rights to family gripes. Rett regaled them with stories of her escapades in Catholic school and beating the boys' team at stickball. Cee-Cee imitated the doctors who swept onto the floor and gave orders without knowing what was going on with their patients. Shiloh kept them laughing with the tale of her first attempt at picking a swell's pocket at ten years old that found her ultimately hiding in a house of ill repute. For her turn, Margot shared the time she and her cousin snuck cigarettes behind a garden shed and set it on fire.

"Just a little scorching," she said as the others giggled like schoolgirls.

Margot noted that neither CeeCee nor Shiloh asked her about her job or her family. Had Rett warned them away from the topics? How could she still feel a camaraderie with these women yet truly know little more about them than their names and their careers? Yet there they were, laughing and chatting like they'd all known one another for years.

CeeCee yawned then laid her hand on Rett's arm. "Sorry, but I'm beat."

She had mentioned she'd worked at the hospital the night before, then had classes earlier today. Margot was impressed that she'd managed to stay upright and cheery.

"Let's get you home." Rett stood, looking at Margot as she and Shiloh rose as well. "You don't have to leave."

"It's been fun, but I should be getting back," Margot said. It *had* been fun, and she wouldn't have traded the evening with them for the world, but eventually they had to return to real life. "I'll find a taxi."

"There's a stand not far from here," Shiloh offered. She nodded to Rett. "You two head home. I'll get her to where she needs to be."

Margot couldn't quite interpret the look on Rett's face. What was she trying to tell Shiloh? A warning not to prod into Margot's business? She doubted Shiloh would give a hoot.

They made their way out of Dumphrey's with shouts of farewell to and from others. Margot didn't know anyone else but got caught up in the smiles and waves. Out on the street, the night had turned chilly.

"We can walk with you," Rett said.

CeeCee yawned again and looped her arm around the investigator's. "It's in the opposite direction from our place.

Shiloh will make sure Margot gets to the taxi stand. Come on, before you have to carry me."

Rett sighed. "Yeah, okay. Good night. Glad you could join us, Margot. We'll talk soon."

Margot grinned at her. "Thank you for inviting me. I had a wonderful time. Just what I needed, like you said. Good night."

As she and Shiloh turned, Margot thought Rett might have mouthed something to the blonde but Shiloh merely waved and smiled and fell into step beside Margot.

She and Shiloh chatted about shows, music, and food as they left the bars, restaurants, and small businesses behind. The merrymaking was still going strong.

Good for them, thought Margot. Though she was glad to be away from the crowded bar, the brisk night air was reviving her. As their walk continued to a more residential area, the streets quieted, with their footsteps marking passage beneath the yellow glow of the gas lamps. Margot was enjoying the walk and the company too much to question the probability that a taxi stand would have been in the busier area they'd left behind.

"Did you and Rett find what you were looking for at that house?" Shiloh asked.

Margot had almost forgotten the magician's assistant had a small inkling of her association with Rett. "We did, thank you."

"I suppose you won't tell me what you two are all about, will you?"

She glanced up at the taller woman. It wasn't easy to read her expression in the lamplight, but Margot hoped Shiloh was teasing more than truly interested.

"It's . . . complicated."

"Most things with Rett are." Shiloh held up her hand. "Don't get me wrong. I love her like a sister. It's just that her line of work is usually . . . complicated."

Margot heard the smile in her voice and relaxed. "That it is."

They walked in silence for a few moments.

"I get the feeling you're more complicated than you appear as well." Shiloh's voice was quiet, not the teasing, fun tone she'd maintained throughout the night.

"Some days." Margot couldn't reveal who she was or how she knew Rett. And the thought of opening up further felt like lead in her stomach. She couldn't let Shiloh know what was going on, because even though Rett trusted the magician's assistant, Margot couldn't. Not with that. "It doesn't matter, does it? I mean, we're getting along well without knowing everything about each other."

"That does have its advantages," Shiloh said.

Margot laughed. "Agreed. Semi-anonymous fun is still fun." She realized Shiloh had stopped walking and turned around. "What's wrong?"

She could just make out Shiloh's strong features, the brightness of her eyes, hands shoved deep into her trouser pockets.

"Nothing's wrong," Shiloh said. "I'm having a wonderful time talking to you, even *not* getting to know you better." Margot smiled at that. "And I don't want it to end."

The bubbly feeling Margot had near the stage door stairs—all evening, truth be told—returned in force. "I'm enjoying being with you too."

"This is my place." Shiloh inclined her head toward the narrow building in front of them. "Here's my question. Do you want to come up, or do you want me to take you to the taxi stand around the corner?"

Rett had been right. Getting out had been exactly what she'd needed. What she felt was *about* to happen was also exactly what she needed.

"Depends on your answer to *my* question," Margot countered, pretty damn sure she already knew the answer. Her heart pounded anyway. "Do you want to kiss me?"

No hesitation. "Very much so."

Blood racing, Margot stepped closer to her. She tilted her head, fingertips brushing the other woman's neck just below her ear, and gently pressed her lips against Shiloh's when she leaned down. She felt Shiloh's hand at her waist, felt the heat of her palm through her dress. They parted without going farther. Though Margot would have been happy to continue, the streets of New York, even after midnight, were not the best place to be caught kissing another woman.

No, there was a much better option, and Margot was all about pursuing the best options. Real life could wait a little longer. "Let's go upstairs."

Eighteen

Sunday morning dawned all too early for Rett. She had promised she'd get down to the city records office early to catch her friend, Sid Hoffmann. Sid wasn't officially working, of course, but he'd be there writing his novel, as he did most every Sunday. Rett had sent him a message yesterday while she was catching up at *her* office before Albert asked too many questions about unresolved tasks.

Rett left CeeCee sleeping and quietly dressed. CeeCee's nursing shift didn't start until two that afternoon, and she deserved all the winks of sleep she could manage.

As she got ready, Rett wondered how Margot and Shiloh had fared Friday night. While she hadn't expected to hear from either of them, they'd been on her mind for the last thirty-six hours.

There was no mistaking Shiloh's interest, but did Margot reciprocate? And would that be a good thing or a bad thing? It was more difficult for Rett to get a read on her than on Shiloh. Margot Baxter Harriman certainly knew how to keep herself to herself.

It's none of your beeswax, Mancini.

Rett left the apartment and locked the door behind her. It wasn't any of her business, or anyone else's, of course. She just didn't want to be in the middle of something awkward. Plus, while she trusted Shiloh completely—well, mostly trusted Shiloh—Margot wouldn't want Shiloh privy to the goings-on with B&H. Not that Rett would share. If they had a "thing" it could get tricky to not talk about Margot. Though Shiloh being Shiloh, any "thing" was likely to be quite casual. Which made some sort of relationship between them, if there was one, only slightly less awkward for Rett if it went sideways.

She sighed heavily at the scenario that wound through her head as she walked to the trolley stop. They were both adults and would sort it out. She couldn't and wouldn't get involved.

The trolley car was less crowded than during the week or even most Saturdays, and Rett managed to find a seat. Transferring a few times took her close to her destination within an hour. She strolled up Chambers Street, then down an alley between the seven-story municipal building and a smaller building. A distant clock struck ten.

The side door where she was to meet Sid wasn't as elaborate as the main entrance to the building, though it had similar ornate ironwork. She glanced up and down the alley to make sure no one had stumbled in. All clear. Rett climbed the shallow stairs and knocked a few times, the door opening in a couple of seconds.

Sid pushed his wire-rimmed spectacles up on his nose. His dirty blond hair was slicked back, his white collar tight, his gray suit neatly pressed. It didn't surprise Rett he looked like he was ready for Monday morning on his day off. He'd always said if one of his superiors ever happened by, he wanted to show his appreciation for them allowing him to use the office by looking responsible. Giving Rett access to the records room notwithstanding.

"Hey, Sid."

"Hey, Rett. Come on in." Sid stepped aside to let her through, then poked his head outside to do his own check of the alley. He shut the door firmly and locked it. "How are things?"

"Good. Mama says hello. She misses you coming over and playing for her and Pop." Sid was quite the pianist. During their high school days, he'd play Chopin before they got down to their homework at the kitchen table. "How about you?"

Sid shrugged as he led her up the stairs. "Same old, same old. Did I tell you Marv and Rachel had their kid?"

"What? No! Mazel tov."

Sid's older brother had been their bane of existence growing up, but now that he was married, Marv had settled down into a reasonable human being. Sid credited Rachel with that.

"Yeah, a boy. Jakob. My parents are over the moon, of course."

"Eases the pressure on you," Rett said. Sid had never been one for romantic companionship of any kind.

Sid laughed. "Thankfully."

When they reached the fourth floor, Sid held the stairwell door open for her. "What are you looking for today? Someone got the bright idea to reorganize, so things might not be where you remember."

Rett took a few seconds to catch her breath. "City directory. Most recent ones you can offer. And maybe census and tax records. Do you have the 1910 census reports?"

Using several sources to corroborate Charles Meade's identity and address would be best, but Rett also knew it was a long shot with such a common name and little else to go on.

"The raw information, yeah, though it's a bit of a mess still." He took her down the hall and unlocked a door.

The room of wood and metal shelves seemed both vast and claustrophobic. Perhaps it was all the deep shadows or that it swallowed up and softened their voices. Sid turned on the lights, long pendant fixtures that hung between rows and rows of almost ceiling-high shelves.

Each set of shelves had a metal ladder attached that rolled along tracks for easier access to the dusty stacks of ledgers and boxes. Each ladder had an attached platform to rest a ledger or box as the seeker went through it, if they didn't want to risk their necks hauling information down the ladder.

"You know the rules," Sid said. "Be careful on the ladder. Don't drop anything. And—"

"And don't put anything back if you take it down," Rett said along with him. Too many times someone unfamiliar with the system had returned a box or ledger to the wrong place, creating all manner of annoyance for the next person in need of it and for the employees charged with finding it.

Sid rolled his eyes at her. "Directories are over there now. Census reports and raw data along the back wall. I trust you to put something back if you stay right there where it belongs, but if you take it to the table you can leave it."

"You know I hate making work for you," Rett said. "You already do so much for me."

"Yes, I do," Sid said, and they both laughed. "I would appreciate it if you'd help me return things when you're done. Or you can invite me over for CeeCee's roast beef some night?"

As a bachelor who didn't cook and lived with two other young men, Sid either went to his family home for meals or ate out. One tended to fray his nerves, the other his wallet.

"Anytime. CeeCee is working most nights, but she'll have Sunday off next week, I think. I'll let you know."

Sid's eyes lit up with anticipation. "That would be swell. Okay, I'd like to be out of here before three, if you can manage that. I'll be up front if you need me."

He headed off around the stacks, to the public desk where he worked during the week.

Rett stared up at the shelves. There was a lot of information in this room. After a few years of working with Albert and grilling Sid and others, she had mostly figured out what resources would work to her advantage. Luckily, each set of shelves had labels on what she could find there.

"Here we go," she said, and dragged the rattling ladder along to start her search.

After three hours, not including the short break where Sid shared his chicken sandwich, Rett had managed to find five potential Charles Meades who worked for the State of New York in some capacity and lived a reasonable distance from the state office that housed the food inspection division.

She had addresses for each; three of them were closer to the office building while the other two were farther afield.

"How are you going to determine the right one?" Sid asked as they put the ledgers back in their proper locations.

"I know he works as a state food inspector, and I have an idea of what he looks like." Rather nondescript from the information Margot had given her. "Otherwise, a few leading questions should do it."

She needed to ask Meade about what he was holding over B&H so she could figure out how to help Margot. Part of the trick would be to get Meade to talk to her without him figuring out who she was or why she was there. She'd need him to lower his guard, to think of her as something completely different. Meade was extorting Margot, which made Rett think he was the sort who would go for being offered something in return for little effort on his part. What would an unmarried, low-paid state employee on the take want other than cash?

Rett glanced at Sid, recalling how he'd wolfed down his lunch. "Do you know where I can get a ham or two around here?"

Rett was down to the last of the three hams she'd purchased. The first had gone to a Charles E. Meade who was sixty-seven and actually had never worked for the State of New York, despite what the tax record said. Charles M. Meade was the right age, and worked for the state, but was a bald, mustachioed plumber. Both men had been thrilled to receive their hams in exchange for answering Rett's completely fictitious "college survey project" questions. Thankfully, they didn't seem to notice she was a little old for a coed.

The last ham would go to Charles P. Meade, whether he was the Charles Meade she needed or not. If he wasn't, she'd get a couple more hams and find the other two tomorrow. It was getting late, her feet hurt, and she was tired of traipsing across the city.

The third Charles lived on the third floor of his building in apartment number three. That seemed like a good sign to Rett as she climbed the last few steps. The five-pound ham felt more like fifty. Who knew hauling pig haunches fifteen blocks, in and out of trolleys, and up and down stairs could be so exhausting?

At apartment number three, she adjusted the strap of her satchel over her shoulder, the weight of the ham causing it to slip again. She listened at the door, but heard nothing. She knocked. Waited. Knocked again, louder.

The door to number four opened, revealing a short, slender man of around her father's age in his shirtsleeves and no shoes. "He ain't in."

Rett affected her college coed smile. "Oh, hello. This is Mr. Charles Meade's home, isn't it? Mr. Meade who works as a food inspector?"

Might as well get right to the point.

"Yeah, but he ain't in."

She kept the smile on her face rather than tell him she'd heard him the first time.

"Do you know when he'll be back? I was supposed to interview him for my college paper and give him this." She dug the wrapped ham out of her bag. "As a thank-you."

The man's eyes locked on the ham. "Don't know. Saw him

head to work Friday, like usual, but haven't heard or seen him since."

Rett frowned. "Not since Friday? You're sure?"

"Thin walls," he said, pointing a thumb back toward his apartment. "Usually he lets me know if he's leaving town. Got fish I feed for him."

"Where does he go?"

The man shrugged. "To his sister's in Westchester somewhere, mostly."

His gaze went back to the ham.

"Oh, bother." Rett didn't have to fake her disappointment even if she censored what she said aloud. "Well, what am I supposed to do with this?"

"I, um, I could hold on to it for him."

"Would you? That would be swell." She handed the ham over. "Do you think you should check on the fish?"

"The what?" He looked slightly dazed for a moment. "Oh, yeah. The fish. I'll ask the landlord to let me in."

"Thanks so much."

The man muttered something as he shut his door, maybe "goodbye," or "here's mud in your eye," or "I have ham." Rett didn't know and didn't care. She made her way down the stairs and out into the quiet Sunday evening.

During the thirty or forty-five minutes it took for her to get back home, she wondered where Charles P. Meade might have gone.

Nineteen

Margot picked absently at the cold toast on her plate while trying not to grind her teeth over Charles Meade and the envelope of cash she would bring him later that morning. There was no set time for her to go by his office, of course. One didn't call for an appointment with their blackmailer. Still, she felt no desire to hurry this particular task, preferring to peruse the Monday morning papers as a distraction and a delay.

She tsk-tsked in sympathy for the victims of the *Titanic* as she read interviews with family members of passengers and crew. Theories abounded about what had happened two weeks before, and the Senate Commerce Committee was determined to get some answers.

Flipping to the next page, Margot groaned as her attention was drawn to an article about the resurgence of illnesses possibly related to foods or medicines. The writer vehemently hoped that the Sherley Amendment would help rein in "corporate shenanigans" exploiting loopholes in the federal law.

She set the paper aside, unable to read any more, her stomach suddenly knotted. So much for distraction.

Sunlight streamed through the large windows, warming the breakfast room. It was usually Margot's favorite time of day, the quiet before the inevitable storm of running a company. Not that things were typically in such an upheaval, but even at the best of times something was going sideways somewhere. It had certainly not been the best of times of late.

She considered a third cup of coffee, but it might be a good idea to eat something more than toast bits. The thought of food, however, wreaked havoc to her stomach.

"Miss Harriman?" Caroline stood in the doorway, hands loosely clasped in front of the white apron over her blue dress. "Mr. Potter is here. Do you want me to show him in, or have him wait in your office?"

Normally, Margot would have had Hiram come through and join her for breakfast. These were not normal times, and definitely not normal conversations to be had.

"The office, please, Caroline. Bring us a fresh pot of coffee, if you would."

"Yes, miss."

Margot stayed at the table, newspapers neatly refolded and set aside, staring out the windows overlooking the back of the house. The vast yard of clipped grass transitioned into another half acre of open pine and birch woodland. The grounds had seen years of garden parties with her parents' friends and associates. Sometimes other children attended, but Margot had never really had friends to invite over until she'd gone to college.

Once she was past the mourning stage for losing her father, and once whatever was going on at B&H had been remedied, she should have a party. Not a business party. She wanted to have fun, to laugh too loud and drink a bit too much. She wanted to invite people she genuinely liked. Rett, CeeCee, Shiloh.

Thoughts of Shiloh and recollection of their Friday night together made her smile despite the anxiety that continued to ripple through her. It had been too long since she'd surrendered to such inclinations, but it was something she'd needed. She'd slept deeply until late Saturday morning, then she and Shiloh had taken their time getting dressed. They'd had a leisurely breakfast at a nearby café before Shiloh saw her off at the taxi stand. Their propriety in public had been diametrically opposed to their physicality the night before.

What would the shareholders think of *that,* she mused.

"Mr. Potter and the coffee are in your office, Miss Harriman."

Reluctantly setting aside more pleasant thoughts, Margot rose with a sigh. "Thank you."

She made her way through the house, noting how quiet it was. How quiet it always was, whether Monday morning or Saturday night. She was getting rather tired of quiet.

Entering the office, Margot saw that Hiram sat in one of the more comfortable chairs across from the desk. She shut the door behind her and hesitated a moment, calming her irritation upon seeing him. He knew something about what Randolph and Mrs. Gilroy had been doing and hadn't shared it with her. Now she was involved and required to give in to Meade's demands or risk everything. Hiram deserved a raised voice, at minimum, but quieter words would be more appropriate at the house. It wasn't that she thought her staff might eavesdrop, but this conversation was not for casual overhearing.

Hiram set his cup and saucer on the desk near the coffee service, then stood to greet her. He wore his typical office attire of a neat, gray pin-striped suit, his thinning hair combed back and his black shoes polished to a mirror-like shine.

"Good morning, Margot."

"Good morning. Please, sit and enjoy your coffee." She started toward the chair before the desk. Should she take a stance as head of B&H? Would it be easier to talk to him, to get to the truth, by confronting him as company president or on friendlier footing?

As much as she cared for him, she wasn't feeling particularly friendly.

Margot poured herself her third cup of coffee of the day and took the seat behind the desk.

Hiram's gray eyebrows lifted as he sat down again. "Something serious, then."

He knew her too well.

Margot wrapped her hands around the coffee cup, realizing how cold they were through the warmth of the china. Her gaze fixed on his face, her stomach gurgled unpleasantly. She had known Hiram her entire life. She thought she knew *him*. He was keeping things from her, and she needed to stop it now.

"Tell me about your meeting with Charles Meade the other day."

If she hadn't been looking for his reaction, Margot might have missed the momentary hesitation as he sipped his coffee.

"Not much to tell. There's been a change in the inspection schedule, is all. I told you that on Friday morning."

"You did," Margot acknowledged, "but when I went to see Mr. Meade Friday afternoon, he had a lot more to tell me."

Hiram reddened with irritation. "You went to see him? Why? I told you it was taken care of. There was no need to bother Meade."

Margot nearly laughed at the absolute gall of the man. Yes, he had been at B&H practically since its inception. Yes, he was her godfather, her father's best friend for decades. But she'd be damned if she'd let anyone risk everything her family had strived to achieve. Even him.

"I wanted some clarification, and since you weren't forthcoming, I decided to go to the source myself."

He set his cup and saucer down on the desk. "I had a busy schedule on Friday, Margot. I would have been happy to give you all the information you wanted when I could. All you had to do was be patient, not go behind my back."

He had a point as far as his schedule was concerned. Hiram had been busy Friday when she tried to talk to him, hurrying off to the advertiser's, then scheduled to leave that evening to attend his nephew's wedding in Philadelphia. Had she been patient enough to wait until today, they could have spoken.

But she hadn't. And what she'd learned from Charles Meade likely would not have been the information he'd have shared.

"All you discussed with Meade was the change in inspection schedule?" she pressed again.

Hiram shrugged. "And new regulations coming in the next year or so. He was kind enough to give me a heads-up so we could start complying and making whatever changes necessary."

His lie came easily, tightening Margot's stomach and pushing the coffee back up her throat.

The state would send such information well ahead of

implementation. There was no need for Meade to have come all the way out to the cannery, and no way the man was simply "passing by" as Hiram had stated. He knew it. She knew it. Did he think she was a fool? Did he think he could sidestep her completely when it came to the goings-on of *her* company?

A small twinge of guilt wormed through her anger. She was thinking like a tyrant. She had only been officially in charge since October and had promised herself she'd consider the experience and expertise of those around her. Hiram had always been so important to her on both personal and professional levels. His investment in B&H was as deep as her own, having given as much or more of himself. He had to have a good reason for keeping things from her.

Please, Hiram . . .

Margot held his gaze, willing him to be the good and honest man she'd known. The man who had brought her caramels. The man who had comforted her in the wake of her father's death. He didn't look away, which would be a sure sign he was trying to hide something. No, he stared right back, as if challenging her to challenge *him*. Because how could she question him, an older, wiser, trusted member of the B&H family who was as close as a blood relative?

And that's what made knowing he was lying to her all the more enraging. All the more painful.

"I spoke to Meade," she reminded him, moving her hands

away from the coffee cup and clasping them together to stop them from shaking. "What else is going on?"

That she already knew slowly dawned in his eyes. His expression changed from indignation to resignation. He broke eye contact, staring into his cup as if he could find excuses in the dregs.

When he didn't produce his own way to explain things, Margot offered hers. "Meade is being paid off. Monthly. Mrs. Gilroy and Randolph had arranged it some time ago, I suspect. But you knew."

Hiram's head came up. He looked resigned, yet something like defiance flashed across his features. "No. Not when it first started."

Margot's fingers clenched. "But you knew eventually. And you weren't going to tell me."

"Of course I wasn't going to tell you, Margot. Don't be ridiculous." His sudden anger caught her by surprise, matching her own. Ridiculous? *She* was being ridiculous? "After Randolph died, Mrs. Gilroy came to me and explained what they'd been doing. I was trying to figure a way out of it without getting you involved."

Months. He'd known everything for months.

And when he hadn't acted in a timely manner, Mrs. Gilroy had decided to inform Margot. That's why she'd let herself into Julia's office to leave the note and not Hiram's. If Hiram were to find it, Mrs. Gilroy likely expected Margot would never see it.

"Meade came by to remind you payment was due." She closed her eyes for a moment, willing herself to calm down, unable to look at the man who had been like an uncle, or even a second father. This hurt went beyond betrayal. He didn't think she could handle what was happening at the company, didn't think she was capable. When she opened her eyes, Hiram was gazing into his coffee cup. "There have been no anomalies in the accounts, Hiram. No odd losses or draining of funds. What's going on? Where's the money coming from?"

She suspected, but she wanted to hear his confirmation. Before he could reply, someone knocked on the door.

"Not now," Margot called out. She was surprised by how steady her voice seemed, because her insides were quivering with equal parts anger and disappointment.

But the person knocking didn't heed the order. The oak door opened. Caroline stood there looking apologetic as she gestured to a figure coming up behind her.

"Forgive the disturbance, Miss Harriman. There's a Lieutenant Presley here to see you. He insisted."

Margot and Hiram locked gazes again. He shook his head slightly as they both stood, either indicating they needed to keep the Meade information from Presley, which was completely obvious to Margot, or that he had no idea why the lieutenant was there either. She had assumed Presley had finished questioning her about Mrs. Gilroy.

Caroline stepped aside to allow Presley, wearing the same brown suit Margot had seen him in when he interviewed her at B&H, into the office. His hat was still on his head and a scowl lined his face. Perhaps Monday wasn't his favorite day of the week. She could relate, particularly on *this* Monday.

"Lieutenant." Margot cleared her throat. "Can I offer you a cup of coffee?"

"No," Presley said gruffly. He looked somewhat abashed at his tone and corrected himself. "No, thank you, Miss Harriman." He nodded to Hiram. "Mr. Potter."

"Has something happened, Lieutenant?" Hiram asked, wiping his nose then slipping his handkerchief back into his pocket.

And did it have anything to do with what Randolph and Mrs. Gilroy had been up to? Margot clasped her hands together in part to cover the tremble that had started and in part to have something to grasp, since her father's neck wasn't available. *How could you get us into this mess, Randolph?*

Presley didn't respond directly. Instead, he addressed Margot. "Where were you Friday night, Miss Harriman?"

Images of the vaudeville show, of laughing with Rett and CeeCee, of smiling until her cheeks ached, of kissing Shiloh, all flashed through her brain as she decided how to answer his question without dragging any of them into whatever was going on.

"I went into the city, saw a show, and stayed with a friend. Why?"

"You had been at the office of Charles Meade earlier that day, correct?" When she didn't reply soon enough for him, he continued. "We have witnesses who said you were in his office and left in a huff, saying something about him not being the best of men."

Not a question, but a statement, and a true one at that. Well, mostly true. As she recalled, she had called him wretched.

"Yes, I went to see Mr. Meade about some regulation changes the state will be implementing and the revised inspection schedule he gave Mr. Potter."

True enough.

"What made you so angry at him?" Presley asked. He wasn't taking notes, and Margot wondered if Meade or someone in the office had complained about her for some reason. Her language, volume, and tone hadn't been ladylike, but it certainly didn't merit a call to the police.

Hopefully, Hiram was willing to corroborate, though she had no idea what Meade might have said or would say to Presley.

"We are heading into our peak season soon, Lieutenant. Making adjustments now and moving up scheduled inspections just aren't feasible. I realize that Mr. Meade's hands are tied, that he's only doing his job, but neither he nor the state can expect miracles."

Margot was somewhat surprised to find herself getting worked up over a conversation that never actually happened.

"Funny you should mention that, Miss Harriman," Presley said.

"Mention what?" Had others assumed that was the gist of her conversation with Meade?

"That his hands were tied. Because that's how he was found."

Margot blinked at him. "What are you talking about?"

Presley's eyes hardened. "Charles Meade was found floating in the bay yesterday with his hands tied and a bullet hole in his skull."

TWENTY

"As you can see, I'm kinda tied up at the moment, Rett." Sergeant Raymond Bittles gestured from behind his high desk in the precinct lobby, directing the coppers and those they'd hauled in. He signed some sort of form, then handed it to a young officer.

The distinct odors of tobacco smoke, sweat, and alcohol told Rett she was not in a particularly "lady-friendly" environment, in case the "accidental" brushing up against her ass by officers and arrested alike wasn't clear enough.

"I know, Ray." She had to speak louder than she wanted to, but those were the breaks when you visited a police station. You'd think a Monday morning would be quieter, but not in

New York. "I was just curious about this body in the bay. Identified as Charles Meade?"

Rett waved the morning paper as if it would spur his memory. The pages had been gripped in her hand since she'd read the story a couple of hours ago. That a Charles Meade had turned up dead after she and Margot had talked about him was not a coincidence. And what a chilling not-coincidence it was.

"Yeah, what about him?"

She lowered the paper. "Which Charles Meade? What did he do for a living? Where did he live? Usually the papers give an address or something. Did he have family? There are . . . there have to be more than a few Charles Meades in this city."

Catching her near misstep, Ray narrowed his gaze at her. "Is there a particular Charles Meade you're worried about?"

There was, but Rett wasn't about to give up more information than she had to. Ray was a good guy, very helpful when he could be, but he was a cop first and foremost, even if he was her brother's oldest friend. If she was asking for specifics, he would want to know why.

"Come on, Ray. I just want to know a tiny detail about him. It's not like I'm asking how he died." Though that would have been useful. "How about you just nod or blink twice if I get something right?"

Ray rolled his eyes. "Yeah, sure. Go ahead."

He would haul her to an interview room if she hit on the

right Charles Meade, so Rett decided to play the odds—and the sinking feeling in her gut—that the dead man *was* the Charles Meade she'd been looking for.

"Did he live at 305 John Street?"

Ray shook his head.

"One twenty-seven Fulton Street?"

Another negative. Those were two of the three Meades she'd visited yesterday and left alive. She asked about the other two she hadn't visited yet and received the same response. That left the absent Charles Meade. There were others in the city, no doubt, but the word "coincidence" had no meaning here.

"Okay. Thanks."

"That's it?" Ray was truly astonished that was all she had asked.

"Yep. I appreciate the help." She started to turn away but he called her back.

"What aren't you telling me, Rett?"

"Nothing. Just checking a few facts." She tried to look innocent, but Ray knew her well and scoffed good-naturedly. May as well push a little more. "One more thing. He was found yesterday, but can you say when he actually died?"

"Friday night or Saturday morning, according to some tests the coroner did." Shouts and the sound of fists hitting flesh grabbed his attention. "O'Brien, get hold of that bastard's arms before he clocks Jeffers again!"

Rett hurried off as Ray moved to help O'Brien and Jeffers with their detainee.

Friday night or Saturday morning.

Margot may have been one of the last people to see him alive.

Or the last if she did it.

The unexpected, unsubstantiated, and unlikely thought stopped Rett in her tracks, causing people to move around her on the sidewalk with not a little grumbling.

Margot had been furious on Friday evening when Rett had been at the house. Furious enough to kill Meade? She certainly didn't seem the type.

But was she the type to hire someone to do her dirty work?

Would a loyal employee like her driver John Bascom do such a thing? Someone else?

Going out with her, CeeCee, and Shiloh gave Margot an alibi. But what about after their time at Dumphrey's?

No. No way. Margot Baxter Harriman wasn't like that. Rett would stake her *own* reputation on that.

But someone else knew about Meade blackmailing B&H. It was very possible they knew Margot now knew. And if they knew Margot, they knew she wasn't one to cave in and continue paying said blackmail, at least not for long.

Which meant B&H and Margot could be in even deeper trouble.

"Shi—shoot." Rett adjusted her expletive when she remembered she was in the middle of a public street, in front of the police station, where some uptight copper might get persnickety about profanity laws.

She needed to talk to Margot.

TWENTY-ONE

Margot could only stare at Lieutenant Presley, her ability to speak hampered by her racing mind. Meade. Found dead. Obviously murdered. And suddenly she knew exactly why the police were in her home: Margot was perhaps the last person to see him alive.

"How awful," Hiram said. "What sort of person does such a thing?"

"We're going to find out." Presley stared back at Margot. "Where were you Friday night and into Saturday morning, Miss Harriman?"

Hiram's gaze bounced between her and Presley. "Surely you can't be serious, Lieutenant?"

"As a heart attack, Mr. Potter. Miss Harriman was recognized as she entered the building, then seen in 'disagreement' with Mr. Meade."

"Disagreement," Margot acknowledged, "not threatening."

At least not out loud.

Presley consulted his notebook. "According to the witnesses, 'The lady'—that would be you—'the lady called him a wretched little man.'" He raised an eyebrow. "They didn't know what you were talking about, but your tone and the slamming of the door tells me you were rather angry."

The telephone on the desk jangled. All eyes went to it, but when Margot met Presley's gaze, he shook his head.

"Leave it. They'll call back."

She sat down gracefully before the wobble in her knees caused her to drop. "I think you're trying to make something out of nothing."

"So make it nothing," the lieutenant said with a shrug. "Both of you tell me where you were Friday night so I can cross you off my list."

"This is ridiculous," Hiram muttered, shaking his head. He glared at Presley. "I left for Philadelphia on the afternoon train. My nephew got married on Saturday. I returned home last night."

The policeman jotted in his notebook. "Witnesses?"

Hiram scoffed. "My entire family. Would that suffice?"

Presley grunted, then looked at Margot. "Miss Harriman?"

Margot cleared her throat. "After I left Mr. Meade's office, I was here until about eight Friday night, then went to a vaudeville show. I stayed in the city until late Saturday morning. Returned about lunchtime. Caroline and John, my housekeeper and driver, can confirm that."

"Of course they can." He didn't sound convinced, though perhaps that was Margot's read of how the police ought to sound. "Which theater? Who did you go with? Where did you spend the night?"

There was no way she could answer his questions honestly and not involve the other women in this mess. She couldn't—wouldn't—do that to them.

"Some little nameless theater off Broadway." Well off Broadway. "A friend recommended it. I stayed with them."

"And this friend's name?"

"I'd rather not get them involved, Lieutenant. We were in a bit of a . . . ahem . . . delicate situation." The heat in Margot's cheeks was due to frustration more than the embarrassment or shame Presley and Hiram would mistake it for.

And there it was.

Hiram flushed and glanced away, shaking his head. Presley's mouth pressed into a thin line. But she would absolutely take advantage of *their* embarrassment for her, a lady of a certain standing, who was implying that she had behaved very unladylike. Why would a lady of certain standing invoke carnal affairs as an alibi if it wasn't true? Of course, they would assume she was with a man.

"I would hope you could take my word that I was otherwise occupied that evening and much of the next day. I had words with Mr. Meade, but nothing more. I'm sure Councilman Lehman can vouch for my integrity, if you wish to ask him. You know Mr. Lehman, don't you?"

Margot hated to bring up Lawrence Lehman, but since the councilman was an acquaintance of the family and the brother of police captain Bart Lehman—Presley's superior—she hoped the connection would have the lieutenant reconsider more probing questions.

Presley harrumphed. He flipped his notebook closed. "Strange that you discovered the body of Mrs. Gilroy at your offices just two weeks before you were seen with Charles Meade, now deceased. And this only months after your own father was found dead, in a very similar situation as Mrs. Gilroy."

His probing gaze met hers unflinchingly, and her mouth went dry. Was he insinuating what she thought he was insinuating?

Margot didn't dare look away from him, or give him any indication that she, too, found the connection between Meade and Mrs. Gilroy strange. But she damn well wouldn't voice any association of Randolph's death to theirs, because there was none. There couldn't be. "Terrible coincidences, Lieutenant."

"Yeah. I don't believe much in those. If something further comes up, I *will* be back. Good day." Presley tipped his hat and abruptly turned around, exiting the office as Amelia came in with the morning post.

Margot thanked the young woman and sorted through the mail while she and Hiram mentally resettled after the lieutenant's visit. The usual correspondence and bills, except for a plain envelope with her name and address handwritten on it. No postmark.

"Honestly, Margot . . ." Hiram's disappointment could have been from her dragging the Lehmans into this, but it was more likely from her admission of spending the night with someone. If he only knew the whole of it.

"I'm not going to apologize for having human needs and feelings, Hiram." She drank her now cold coffee. "But I'll try to be more careful next time and not have you aware of my more personal activities."

"Thank you." He sighed heavily. "If you'd only—"

Margot held up her hand, palm out. "Don't say it. Do not say, 'If you'd only get married.'" It was a familiar refrain she'd heard in the dozen years since graduating college. "I'm perfectly content as I am."

Should she marry, much of the autonomy she enjoyed would evaporate. She wasn't about to let that happen.

"I'm concerned about you having companionship, is all."

"Obviously 'companionship' isn't a problem." She laughed

at the stricken expression on his face. "You're concerned that my dalliances, infrequent as they are, will make B&H look bad. They haven't so far, Hiram, and as long as the police don't question them, I take care to assure they never will. If I were a man, you'd be applauding my conquests."

"But you aren't a man, Margot. Society is what it is. I'm just trying to protect you and all we've worked for."

He was, in his way.

"I know, and I appreciate that." She refreshed her coffee with a little more cream and sugar. "I'll be more careful. At least until society allows me equal freedoms."

He grunted in resignation or disbelief. It was hard to tell. She certainly wasn't holding her breath waiting for men to decide she was equal to them.

"At least we won't have to pay Meade anymore," Hiram said into his cup.

Margot hadn't particularly liked the man, but he hadn't deserved to be murdered. And Hiram's words only reinforced her doubts about *him*. Was Meade's murder connected to her and B&H? Presley certainly seemed to think so. But how?

As Margot took a letter opener to the mail, something Hiram had said to Presley whirled through her brain. Hiram had left town for the weekend, but he'd originally planned to leave later in the evening, after supper, not in the afternoon as he'd told the lieutenant.

Margot peered at him, hands stilled with the brass opener

in one and the unmarked envelope in the other, only half listening to her godfather telling her about projected farm yields, schedules, and personnel requirements.

Had he taken the earlier train to Philadelphia, or had he only said as much—giving himself an alibi—and gone into the city to speak to Meade after she had left?

She didn't think Hiram had killed Meade, but there was something he was hiding from her. Surely he didn't expect her to have forgotten their discussion just because they'd been interrupted by Presley.

"You never told me where the money was coming from."

Hiram stopped in the middle of his suggestion that they hire a new advertising agency. "I'm sorry?"

"Before Presley came in, I asked you about the money that my father had Mrs. Gilroy use to pay off Meade. You said she spoke to you about it."

She waited for him to talk about the fake medical reimbursements for the fake employees that had fake injuries at the very real B&H facilities that cost them very real money given to a very real, now dead man.

"Yes. Right. Mrs. Gilroy. They were falsifying medical claims. Cash withdrawals from a general fund account small enough not to cause a ruckus."

Not taken from Randolph's personal account because Margot saw to those statements since her mother had passed away. They knew she'd question regular withdrawals.

Simple fraud. She figured as much, and it was good to have that confirmation, but there was something else. Something about people being hurt that Mrs. Gilroy mentioned in her note. She couldn't have been talking about the "injured" workers. From what Margot could tell from the few files she'd found, those "employees" probably didn't even exist, so neither did their injuries. Who was Mrs. Gilroy talking about? More confounding, what was Hiram trying to spin?

"She was using the money to pay Meade."

"Of course," Hiram said as if it was obvious. "Did you think she was taking it for herself? You know how some get an inkling of power and have to profit from it. Meade threatened to give us bad reports if we didn't pay, so Randolph paid. It's practically on par with wining and dining suppliers during price negotiations."

Practically, but not quite.

"Taking money out of the company accounts through the false claims." Illegal and unethical as it was, it made sense, tied up into a neat little package. Too neat. "Anything else?"

His gaze darted across the desk and landed on the coffeepot.

"No." Lying through his teeth, he poured himself another cup of coffee.

Damn him.

She needed to figure out how to get him to tell her everything Mrs. Gilroy had shared.

While she considered tactics, Margot opened the handwritten envelope and removed the folded paper.

Meade is gone, but your debt isn't. $50,000 under the Bronx River Gate at the zoo by 5 P.M. *Friday. Come alone. Do not linger. Or EVERYONE will know what B&H did.*

Twenty-Two

Rett heard her father's heavy footsteps coming down the hall just as Margot's housemaid on the other end of the phone told her Miss Harriman was unavailable. Rett had tried Margot's home office phone, but no one answered.

"Please have her call Rett. She's got the number. Thanks."

Rett dropped the receiver onto the holder half a second before Albert entered the office and picked up the morning mail. "Hey, Pop."

Albert turned to shut the door, his movements slow and stilted. When had that started? He swept his hat off his head, smoothed back his thick white hair, and started to unbutton his coat as he walked past her. "Where were you earlier?"

No greeting. Little eye contact. That was becoming standard. Albert had never been a demonstrative parent, but he'd at least said hello to her most of the time.

Not that he didn't have the right to question her. She had been late to the office this morning after visiting the police station, though not all that late. She beat him in by at least half an hour on the days he was supposed to come in. Had he been by and found the door locked? Sometimes he forgot his keys at home. Maybe he'd called and got no answer.

"I was prepping for the Klimmel case." Not true, but she would be doing that this afternoon to make up for time taken while at B&H last week. "Did you need me to do something else?"

Getting dirt on cheating husbands wasn't her favorite aspect of the job, though it paid the bills. She just hoped whatever Albert might have for her could wait until she was done with the B&H job.

"No, I just expect you to be here when you're supposed to be here." He shoved his office door open hard enough for it to bang against the wall and shrugged out of his coat. "You disappeared last week and have nothing on the Klimmel case? What am I paying you for? To go out and get your hair done?"

Heat blossomed in Rett's chest and crawled up her neck. She'd learned to recognize one of Albert's "moods," but this was different. Admittedly, she'd put off following Klimmel around, but the man wasn't going to suddenly change his routine. He'd still be schtupping his secretary this coming week. And the crack about getting her hair done? Uncalled for.

"I'm a bit behind on some tasks, that's all."

"Maybe you shouldn't have them at all." Albert hung up his hat and coat on the rack just inside his door and turned around, arms crossed, glaring at her. "If it's too much for you, I'll hire someone else to do it."

He didn't mean a second assistant.

She had tried to be more patient with him, had even asked Mama the best ways to keep him calm, but something inside her snapped.

Rett rose, hands fisted at her sides. "First off, I can and will get them done. Like I always do. Second, you can't afford to hire anyone *but* me."

His gaze narrowed. "What the hell is that supposed to mean? You get paid plenty for a woman."

"'For a woman'? What the hell does *that* mean?" She knew better than to goad him, yet the words flew out of her mouth. "Like I don't have expenses? Like I don't have to pay rent or buy food?"

"If you were married, you wouldn't have to worry about that."

Rett mimicked his crossed arms. "Well, I'm not, and I have no plans to be, so maybe I should be paid what you'd pay a man. That way you won't have to worry about me moving back home half starved."

Albert's bushy eyebrows drew together in a frown. "You aren't getting married, ever? What are you going to do, live with that girl the rest of your life?"

Yes.

"CeeCee and I are happy with our arrangement." They were more than happy, and it tore Rett up inside because she couldn't share that happiness with him.

"What if she finds a husband, some doctor? What then?" He was sneering at this point, so sure of his view of the world, of her.

"She won't."

"Sure she will. She's pretty. She's smart. A nice doctor will take care of her."

"She's studying to be a doctor herself, you know," Rett reminded him. He scoffed. Her temperature went up and her fists tightened, fingernails digging into her palms. "She won't go off and marry a man because she loves *me,* Pop. Me. And I love her."

Albert's jaw dropped open.

The very air seemed to solidify, freezing them both in place.

Damn it. This was not the way Rett had wanted to tell him about her and CeeCee. Part of her had hoped he'd get the idea;

he was a detective, after all. But either they had been good at keeping their secret or he had chosen not to see it.

"Does your mother know?" he asked, his voice low and raspy. As if he could barely get the words out.

"Yes. She figured it out pretty much the first time CeeCee came over for Sunday dinner." Rett swallowed a snippy comment about hiring Mama as a partner in the business.

"Get out." His words were quiet but hit her in the gut and heart like bullets.

"What? Pop, I—"

"Get. Out."

Rage and sadness lodged in her chest, choked off expletives and pleas she wanted to hurl. She turned around and walked stiffly to the coatrack to retrieve her things. Not bothering to take the time to put them on, Rett left the Mancini & Associates office with a gentle click of the door latch.

Twenty-Three

Margot's heart thudded hard against her sternum. She stared down at the paper, blinking a few times to make sure she'd read it correctly. Much like the note from Mrs. Gilroy, the words burned into her brain.

"Margot? Are you all right?" Hiram's voice sounded as if it was coming from far away.

She lifted her head. His concern seemed genuine. It always seemed genuine. But was it? How could she trust him? How could she trust anyone?

"I'm fine," she lied. Those two words often were lies as of late. *Don't let them see you flinch.* She folded the paper and slid it back into the envelope. "What were you saying?"

"I was saying we can get the accounts audited, if you'd like, but that will take time. Are you sure you're all right? Did you get some bad news?" He glanced at the envelope and his face paled. "Something else we need to worry about?"

"No." *Liar.* She slid the envelope back among the others and set the pile aside.

What were they discussing? Audits. Reconciling accounts against the monies Mrs. Gilroy and her father had siphoned to Charlie Meade.

"Yes, an audit. Have Julia start procedures this week. I want to bring in someone unaffiliated with B&H or the family," she said, sounding nearly normal in her ears. "An independent accountant. They won't need to know why we're doing it. Julia will assist them as necessary."

"Of course." He sipped his coffee, agreeable and calm as could be, except for the shadows under his eyes. Shadows of what? Lack of sleep due to concern? Deceit? Guilt?

Margot watched him over the rim of her cup, her hands trembling less than she'd expected considering what she'd just read. "Is there anything else, Hiram? Other than the medical fraud?"

He hesitated. She thought he was going to say something. Instead, he drained his cup and set it on the desk. Hiram stood up, taking a handkerchief from his pocket. He dabbed his face and wiped his nose. When he put the handkerchief away, his blue eyes looked clearer. He'd made a decision.

"No, nothing else."

Disappointment pierced her chest as if it were a knife. *Why?* she wanted to ask. *Why are you lying to me? Why are you keeping things from me?*

And though she had every right to ask, her throat closed around the words before she could get them out.

He still treats you like you're a child, and you still treat him like he's the hero you grew up with.

"I'll see you at the office later, and we can decide on an independent accountant." He turned and walked stiffly to the door, closing it behind him and leaving her alone.

Margot closed her eyes as a piece of her heart seemed to fall away. Why hadn't she confronted him about her doubts? Why hadn't she told him about the blackmail note sitting among the bills and invitations?

Because she wasn't sure she could trust Hiram Potter to answer truthfully anymore. And the idea of losing him as a dear friend, as a father figure, as a member of a very small circle of people she thought she could rely upon, hurt almost as much as losing her parents.

Twenty-Four

Rett shut the passenger-side door and waved Bascom goodbye as he drove off to park the car elsewhere on the Harriman grounds. She'd luckily gotten through to Margot by using the telephone of one of the other office building occupants. When she told her now only employer they needed to talk, Margot had immediately offered to send her car and driver to pick her up.

As clouds gathered over the city, Rett walked up to the double front doors. She had to shake off her conversation with Albert and focus on the Harriman case. On the drive over, she had nearly sobbed on poor Bascom's shoulder at the thought that Albert will have likely forgotten their entire exchange by tomorrow while she still felt its sting. Gruff and difficult as he could be, Rett missed her father more and more each day.

Rett rang the doorbell. She breathed in the charged air, the sweet anticipation of a coming storm. She'd rather be home, curled up under a blanket with a cup of tea in one hand, a good book in the other, and CeeCee's head resting on her thigh.

Thinking about how Albert would react to such a scene sent equal parts of anger and grief through her again.

Not now, she admonished herself, swallowing to loosen the constriction in her throat.

A young woman opened the front door, eyes bright and questioning. She wore the black-and-white uniform of a housemaid. "Yes?"

"I'm Loretta Mancini, here to see Miss Harriman. She's expecting me."

"Of course, Miss Mancini. Come in." She opened the door wider to allow Rett into the foyer. "Miss Harriman is in her office."

"Thank you, um . . . ?"

The girl smiled. "Amelia, miss. Can I take your hat and coat?"

Rett passed the garments to her, but kept her satchel.

Amelia draped the coat over her arm. She led the way to the office door and knocked. When a muffled "Yes?" sounded, Amelia opened the door just enough for her head and upper body to pass through. "Miss Harriman, Miss Mancini is here for you."

"Show her in," Margot said.

Amelia opened the door wider and, smiling, gestured for Rett to enter the well-lit office.

"Thank you." Rett passed her and strode to one of the chairs before the desk.

"Hello, Rett. Can I offer you some coffee?" Margot stood near her desk. Papers were strewn about, and a small black book with a pencil holding it open on a particular page rested on the vast walnut surface. "Better yet, lunch." She addressed Amelia. "Can we have some sandwiches and tea, please?"

"Yes, Miss Harriman." Amelia closed the door.

Margot brought her attention to Rett again and the calm expression she'd maintained for the maid shifted to concern. "Come sit down. What's happened? You sounded terrible on the telephone."

Rett had tried to keep herself together while she called Margot a second time, unwilling to let the office neighbor see or hear her grief. But Margot had heard it through miles of wire.

"It's—" She nodded toward the sideboard where Margot kept the decanter of whisky. "Can I have a glass of that, please?"

"Of course." Margot made her way around the desk and poured each of them a finger, then added another finger to each glass. She handed one to Rett.

"Thanks." Rett threw back half of the drink in one gulp, clearing her thoughts with the burn in her throat and sinuses. She closed her eyes for a moment, breathing deeply. "Thank you."

Margot motioned for her to have a seat, sitting in the matching chair across from Rett. She sipped her drink. "What happened?"

Rett shook her head, not wanting to discuss what had prompted her to drink so early in the day, but the words spilled out anyway. "Albert. He was angry I hadn't been in earlier, then we got into an argument over what he's paying me, and how I don't need money 'cause I'm only a woman, after all, and if I was married I wouldn't have to worry about it."

"Oh, boy."

"Yeah."

"I'm sorry. I know it can be hard." Margot had mentioned her own father had been difficult to deal with, particularly as he became ill. It helped that she knew what Rett was going through.

"Then I opened my big mouth." Rett sat down. "I lost my temper, said things. It wasn't good. I'd rather not go into it."

She felt a little guilty not telling Margot that Albert had essentially fired her. Until it was official—and she'd determine that in the next few days—she'd continue with the B&H investigation. And keep her fingers crossed.

Margot nodded slowly. "Understood. I'm here if you need an ear."

"Thank you." Rett cleared her throat and took another sip of whisky. It went down much easier than the gulp. "Have you heard about Meade?"

Margot swallowed the rest of her drink and immediately rose to refill her glass. Her clenched fist and stiff gait meant whatever had happened here wasn't good either.

"Margot?"

When she turned around, Margot seemed paler, with lines etched around her eyes and mouth that Rett hadn't noticed before. "Lieutenant Presley showed up while I was here talking to Hiram. He said Mr. Meade was found with his hands tied, shot in the head."

"My God."

Rett figured Meade had been murdered, but tied up and shot? That sailed past a confrontation gone wrong and smack into premeditated territory. A shiver ran down her spine. Things had taken a turn, moving beyond simple blackmail.

"That wasn't in the paper," she said. "My friend at the police station was reluctant to give more information. I'm sure they want to hold back details while they look for the killer." She joined Margot at the sideboard. "This has gotten nasty, Margot."

Margot tossed back a finger of whisky. "I know."

She returned to the desk, sorted through a stack of envelopes, chose one, and handed it to Rett.

Curious, Rett examined the writing and envelope. Nothing fancy about the script or the paper. Small but legible writing. No postmark. It had to have been hand-delivered. She glanced at Margot.

"Open it," she said, her voice strained. Whatever was in the envelope, it wasn't an invitation to the Governor's Ball.

Rett took out the single page and read. Then read it again to make sure the words were correct. Her heart nearly beat itself out of her chest. She sat down, shaking her head. "Holy Hannah. When did you get this?"

"It was with this morning's post."

"What are you going to do?"

"For the moment, keep it quiet, like everything else, and consider how to scrape up fifty thousand dollars without letting anyone know." Margot took the note from her and slid it into the top drawer. "Presley asked us not to say anything about Meade. If it gets out, I suppose he'll know who to blame. He also wanted to know where I was Friday night and Saturday morning."

Rett had her suspicions. It was none of her business, but she also wanted to know if and how she may have fit into Margot's alibi. "What did you tell him?"

"That I was out at a show with a friend, then spent the night in the city with said friend." Margot's chuckle was without humor. "No names or details, though he came to his own conclusions, faulty as they may have been. Hopefully, he won't be back to ask more."

Rett shifted on the chair, but her gaze never wavered. "Can *I* ask where you were after CeeCee and I left Dumphrey's?"

"Do you think I killed Meade?" Her dark eyes glinted with something akin to a challenge. No, not a challenge, more like a test. She *wanted* Rett to ask the hard questions.

"No." Rett sipped her whisky. "Your private life is your own. Forget it. I shouldn't have asked."

"No, it's all right," Margot said. She took a breath, as if girding herself for Rett's reaction. "To put your mind at ease, I was with Shiloh."

Rett let out a short bark of laughter, nodding. "That explains why you couldn't tell Presley the whole truth." She finished her drink and muttered, "Ridiculous laws."

"You don't seem surprised we were together."

"Margot, I watched the two of you Friday night." She grinned, recalling their furtive glances and "accidental" hand brushings. "I would have been more surprised if you hadn't gotten together."

Color rose along Margot's neck and cheeks. "Oh. I thought I was hiding it well enough."

"You were. Shiloh is terrible about keeping things like that to herself. She's great on stage and keeping professional secrets, but get her with a pretty woman and it's all over her face. To put *your* mind at ease, you were harder to read."

They both laughed, and Rett felt some of the tension ease from her shoulders. Speaking to someone else who understood her felt good. It had been too long since she'd been able to have such an open conversation.

Margot held the crystal glass between her palms. "So, um, you and CeeCee?"

"Almost three years," Rett said, smiling. "Just about since the day we met at the hospital. People don't think too hard about two single working women sharing a place. We're careful out in public, of course." Her smile faltered. "That's the other part of what Albert was upset about. I told him about me and CeeCee."

Sympathy furrowed Margot's brow. "I'm sorry, Rett. I do understand how difficult it is to be yourself to the rest of the world. Or even to those you love."

Having learned more about Margot, Rett knew her empathy was genuine. "That explains why you haven't been connected to New York's most eligible bachelors."

Margot laughed again and rolled her eyes. "They've tried, believe me. I'll dance with one or two men at functions, getting tongues to wag, but for the most part New York society has deemed me the spinster heiress, too caught up in business to have a 'real' life. There has been speculation about who I'll leave my controlling shares of B&H to once I'm gone."

Rett was curious, but she wouldn't ask, and the other woman didn't elaborate.

"But none of that matters at the moment," Margot continued. "What did you call about earlier?"

Right. The real reason she was here. Having a friendly ear and shoulder in Margot Harriman would help her focus.

"I had tracked down Meade's address yesterday and went to visit. His neighbor said he hadn't been home all weekend." Rett made a face. "Now we know why."

"Indeed." Margot sipped the last of her drink, wincing not over the bite of the liquor, Rett figured, but over Meade's fate. "What were you going to do if you had found him?"

She shrugged. "Try to figure out what his angle was. How he could get at you and your company."

"That would have been helpful." Margot's sigh of frustration echoed Rett's feelings. They hadn't gotten much in the way of real answers. "People have been hurt. Someone has been killed. And the blackmail has reached a whole new level. We need to stop this."

"Unless the murderer was you or Hiram, it was someone who knew that Meade was blackmailing B&H, and why."

Understanding dawned on Margot's face, along with renewed worry. And anger. "An accomplice? What would cause them to murder their own? Though there is that adage of no honor among thieves."

Rett had heard that often enough. "If we figure out who

killed Meade, we'll be able to connect more dots. Or vice versa."

"Is it possible his murder wasn't connected to blackmailing B&H?" Margot suggested. "We don't know anything about Meade. He could have been into all manner of things, targeting other companies."

"He wasn't living the life of a man with that sort of cash flow, though I could do a lot with an extra hundred smackers a month. Unless he had a hell of a bank account somewhere, we'll have to assume the singular connection with B&H. That he died not long after talking to you and Potter is too much of a coincidence for my liking. I don't believe in coincidences." Rett took a notebook and pencil from her satchel, set them on the desk, then removed her spectacles from a hard case and fitted them over her ears. "What do we know about Meade?"

Margot leaned back in her chair, a thoughtful expression on her face. "He'd been with the Division of Food Safety and Inspection for about ten years, so before federal laws. From my few encounters with him, he was always pleasant and easy to work with, until Friday."

Rett snorted. "Considering he was being paid off each month for who knows how long, sure." She glanced up at Margot. "Sorry. I learned he'd been in the same apartment for at least as long as he'd been with the state, that he has a pet fish, and his sister lives somewhere in Westchester County. The neighbor said he visited her sometimes."

"Meade had some sort of framed citation on his office wall from the Yonkers Chamber of Commerce and a diploma from a school there."

Rett jotted notes. "So he's likely from the area." She tapped the pencil on the edge of the book. "Something..."

"What?"

"The truck driver I saw at the can-making building. The company is up in Yonkers."

"Many are," Margot said.

"Yeah, but there seem to be a few lines leading up to that neck of the woods. Also, the driver brought a gun into Mrs. Gilroy's, and Meade was shot. I'm not saying it was him, but I wouldn't rule him out, either. Hired thugs often have various skills."

"A gun?" Surprise flitted across Margot's face. "You didn't tell me he had a gun that night."

"Sorry, I was more concerned with getting us out of there at the time. The question is, who could have hired him for both tasks? It would have to be someone who knows what's going on at B&H. Someone with money." Rett studied her notes. Who had those two things going for them? She didn't like where her conclusions led, and she was damn sure the woman sitting on the other side of the desk would like it even less. "Margot, my dots connect to Hiram Potter."

Margot said nothing, her mouth pressed into a thin line. There was no shock, no surprise. No denial.

"You think so too." Rett saw a flicker of pain in the other woman's eyes. Of course she didn't want to believe a longtime friend was involved. But she already had proof her own father and another friend had been involved in whatever was going on. Another hit to Margot's trust may have been too much. "I'm sorry."

A sad smile barely curved her lips. "Don't be. I thought the same thing when he said there was nothing other than medical fraud. Mrs. Gilroy's note to me didn't refer to that, though, and I think Hiram knows what it *does* refer to even if he won't say." Her features clouded. "I thought I knew him, but now, I'm not so sure."

She shook her head. Her feelings of betrayal were palpable. Rett could sympathize.

"Is he being overly protective or covering his own ass?"

"Both? I don't know. I hope to God it's more the former." Margot's jaw tightened and her expression grew stormy. "What's important is getting to the bottom of this. I told you from the first day we met that I wanted to know the truth, no matter who was involved. Even if it's Hiram."

TWENTY-FIVE

After they ate the soup and sandwiches Amelia brought in, Margot and Rett went through the B&H files once again. Between the cabinets in the office and those in the basement, they discovered four more questionable medical reimbursement payments and receipts. Now that they were aware of the Martin Scrap & Metal Fabrication's driver, regular payments to them over the last few years were pulled as well.

"That's quite a bit," Rett said, wiping sweat from her brow.

"We've been buying metal from them pretty much since we started making our own cans." Margot put her hands on her hips, leaning back and to the sides to stretch her muscles.

"That was nearly five years ago, though the dates on these medical files only go back a couple of years."

Rett pulled out the papers she had found in Mrs. Gilroy's safety-deposit box. "The dates here that seem to be payments for Meade are only a couple of years old. Which makes sense. They didn't start the medical fraud until Meade started his demands. I'm still not sure how Martin's is involved, other than the driver."

"One thing keeps coming up, though."

Rett nodded. "Meade. The bakery. The Martin's driver. They all have Yonkers in common. Far enough away to be left to their own devices, but close enough to coordinate whatever needs to be coordinated. Though you may have personnel up there who are involved."

The thought made Margot's stomach turn.

"But," she continued, "the general guideline is to have only as many folks as necessary aware of the grift. Too many hands in the pot to pay off and too many mouths that can run is bad business."

A humorless laugh escaped Margot. "Well, that's comforting."

Rett's wry smile told her the investigator understood her frustrations. "If it were simply someone stealing from the company, I think you'd feel better, in a sense. I know this is hitting close, touching a nerve."

Margot could only nod in agreement, her throat suddenly

tight. Anger, sadness, betrayal, concern, all balled up together in her stomach, threatening to reject her lunch. She could see no way to save her company until they figured out who was responsible. And they needed to do it before the blackmailer's Friday drop-off deadline.

After a moment, she asked, "What's the next step?"

"A trip to Yonkers. I'll look into the metal shop and your bakery there. See if I can link Meade to either of them. And maybe how Hiram Potter might be involved, other than in an official capacity. He doesn't seem to have any other connection, but best to check it out." Rett must have seen anguish Margot had tried to conceal, for the younger woman's expression softened. "We have to make sure either way, Margot. At the very least, I'll try to confirm that your people up there aren't involved."

That would be some relief, anyway.

"How do you plan to get information from the bakery? Do you want me to write you some sort of letter?" Though a stranger's visit to the bakery could ignite suspicions from the staff, she couldn't see any other way to get Rett access to the facility.

"No, too risky. We don't want any connection between you and me." Margot could almost see the wheels of Rett's thoughts turning. She was onto something. "You have the letter from Meade about inspections. Can I borrow that?"

"Of course. Can I ask why you need it?"

"A letter from the State of New York regarding a surprise inspection would get me in to see the place and talk to the manager, maybe check records, correct?" Rett smiled when Margot acknowledged that to be true. "All I need is something for Shiloh's dad to copy. It'll look as official as the real thing."

Margot wasn't sure if she should be impressed or concerned that such things as counterfeiting official documents weren't as difficult to pull off as she'd thought. At least it was working to Margot's advantage.

"I'll get the letter to you tomorrow."

Margot asked Bascom to see her in her office after he took Rett home. She had just finished a soothing cup of chamomile tea when she heard him knock on the door.

"Come in."

Bascom entered, then shut the door behind him. He must have hung up his hat and coat in the back closet of the house, the entrance he usually used to access the garage. His suit was as fresh-looking as the moment he'd put it on in the morning, though Margot saw lines of weariness around his eyes as he drew closer.

"You wished to see me, Miss Harriman?"

Margot smiled and gestured for him to sit in one of the chairs across from her. "John, you've known me pretty much all my life. Will I ever get you to call me Margot?"

He grinned as he sat down, somehow looking relaxed and formal at the same time. "Probably not, miss."

She laughed and shook her head. Old habits and disciplines were hard to break, she supposed.

He patiently waited for her to gather herself and get to it.

"Did you take Hiram Potter to the train station on Friday?" It wasn't often that Hiram asked for Bascom, but Margot knew he preferred not to leave his vehicle at the train station.

"No," Bascom replied. "I brought Miss Mancini here, then took the two of you into the city. I haven't driven for Mr. Potter in several months. I mean, outside of when you ride together."

"Do you happen to know how he got to the station Friday and when?"

"No, miss. I saw him when I brought you to the cannery at noon, though."

Margot sat up. "You did?"

"Yes. I was in the car, reading the newspaper." Bascom looked thoughtful. "He ran out of the building and caught up with another gentleman. Mr. Potter seemed rather agitated. I couldn't hear what they were saying, but judging by the look on both their faces, it was not a pleasant conversation. The other man—I don't know who he was—poked his finger into Mr. Potter's chest. I thought someone was going take a swing and was getting ready to step in when the other man walked away."

"This other man," Margot said, "what did he look like?"

Bascom described Charles Meade, or someone who looked an awful lot like him.

Hiram and Meade. Arguing outside of B&H. About what? Not the supposed change in inspection schedule. According to Hiram, that was business as usual.

"What did Mr. Potter do next?"

"He got into his Model T. His face was so red, Miss Harriman, I thought he was going to have a heart attack then and there." Bascom shook his head. "But he sat in his car for a minute, like he was collecting himself, then drove off."

If Margot hadn't gone to see Meade not long after, she would have been more than half convinced Hiram had hunted him down. Maybe he had, finding the food inspector before taking a later train to Philadelphia instead of the afternoon one. Or hiring the metalworks' truck driver to do the deed.

She shook her head. No, she couldn't believe Hiram Potter would do that. Any of that.

Could he?

"Miss Harriman, are you all right?"

Margot brought her gaze up from her fisted hands on the desk to look at him. "I'm fine. Just . . . thinking. Thank you. Sorry to keep you up so late."

Bascom rose. "Not a problem, miss. Anything you need. Good night."

"Good night."

After he left, Margot tipped the decanter of whisky into her teacup, adding a generous dollop. Hiram never told her or Lieutenant Presley he'd argued with Meade. Not a word. Was it because it wasn't a big deal, or because he knew it would look bad?

After what she and Rett had worked out earlier, the latter seemed to be the case.

Was it possible that, in his effort to protect B&H from blackmailers, Hiram Potter was involved in Meade's brutal murder? He had always been the soft-spoken uncle sort, yet fiercely loyal to B&H and her father. Would that loyalty still apply to her if she pushed against what he thought was best for the company? If he'd killed—God, the very idea!—one man to maintain B&H, was she as safe as she thought?

TWENTY-SIX

The train arrived at the Putnam Line Getty Square station on the north side of Yonkers's Washington Park just before ten on Wednesday morning. With new industries, businesses, and housing cropping up, Rett was having a tough time telling where the Bronx stopped and Yonkers began.

A new Central Railroad station with a luxurious interior had recently opened on Buena Vista to accommodate the ever-growing city, the conductor had proudly told her. Rett made the appropriate positive responses.

Maybe she and CeeCee could holiday here or farther upstate one of these days. Thinking they'd need to coordinate days off made Rett snort a sad laugh. Her continued employment at Mancini & Associates depended on Albert's state of mind.

But for now, she *was* employed, and determined to do her best for Margot Harriman.

Rett descended from the train and hurried through the station near Getty Square. She opened her umbrella and joined the few pedestrians brave enough to face the weather. Rain fell in sheets, the occasional clap of thunder shaking the very air.

Stepping off to the side of the walk, she stopped to get her bearings. According to the directions Margot gave her, the B&H bakery was almost due east, off Edwards Avenue. Rett sniffed the air, hoping to catch a whiff of the delicious aroma that accompanied such establishments, but the air was full of acrid smoke and damp scents instead.

The Martin Scrap & Metal Fabrication facility was likely to the west, near the industrial docks on the Hudson. She'd catch a trolley to get closer to them later.

"To the bakery it is," she said aloud.

No one paid her much mind as they moved past, their umbrellas dripping and their feet squelching in puddles. Rett smiled. Yonkers *was* getting to be more like the city.

She walked up South Broadway, toward Getty Square, then turned right down Main Street. The Getty House on the corner was as grand as anything in Manhattan, and she made a mental note to check the luncheon menu before she returned home. CeeCee's birthday in the fall would be a great time for a short getaway and a few fancy meals.

Rett continued east on Main Street, then crossed the bridge over the Nepperhan River to Edwards Avenue. Ah! There it was. The soothing scent of baked goods.

The B&H bakery wasn't open to retail sales, which meant very little foot traffic around the building. So little that Rett had a bit of a time finding the door to the reception area around the side of the building. Barging in through the EMPLOYEES ONLY door would definitely start her off on the wrong foot. But find it she did, taking a moment to smooth her hair and shake rainwater off her umbrella before going in.

The small public area was decorated with grainy photographs of trucks with B&H logos painted on the sides, smiling groups of people holding up loaves of bread, and mustachioed men in white aprons standing beside a horse-drawn wagon. A desk with a telephone was unattended. Of the two interior doors, one was closed, perhaps leading into the workings of the bakery, and the other was ajar. Soft scuffing sounds came from that room.

Rett called out, "Helloooo?"

Something thudded. "Damn it. Just a minute!"

There was nothing interesting on the desk, and the squat cabinet in the corner was too close to the door. Rett didn't want to risk getting caught snooping.

The person in the other room muttered several indistinguishable words, then came out. A gangly man about her age with a neat mustache, wearing a blue suit, closed the door, smiling at Rett with prominent front teeth.

"Hello. What can I do for you?"

Rett returned the smile. "My name is Sarah Smith. I'm with the state's Factory Investigating Committee." She presented the letter Mr. Wallace had forged for her, complete with the state seal and a bogus letter of introduction and intent signed by one utterly fictitious Hamish K. McGuire. "I'm here to look at your health and safety practices, particularly pertaining to employee injuries and fatalities."

The man blinked at her, the smile frozen on his face. "But you're . . . a woman."

Rett held back a retort regarding his observation skills. "Yes, I am. The state has launched a new hiring program for young women. I can relay your thoughts about it, if you'd like. After we're done."

He held out his hand. Mentally crossing her fingers, she gave him the letter. He snapped it open, perusing the absolute lie on the page with several hums.

He returned the letter to her. "I see. Well, Mr. Clary, the manager, isn't in today."

What luck. She would only need to convince this man.

"Oh, no. But I'm sure you can help me. I just need to see employee medical claims and corresponding employment files for the past five years." Rett affected her best damsel-in-distress face. "Please. I have to get back to Mr. McGuire by this afternoon or he'll be steamed. It won't take long."

He glanced over his shoulder at the closed door. "I suppose."

She lit up and clasped her hands to her chest. "Oh, thank you so much, Mister . . . ?"

"Barby. Franklin Barby."

Rett stuck out her right hand. "Mr. Barby. I'm Sarah Smith. But you knew that."

"I did." Barby shook her hand gently, but when she tried to pull out of his grasp, he tightened his hold. "So, what's in it for me?"

Something tripped in Rett's chest. "I beg your pardon?"

Gone was the hesitant, uncertain young man. In his place, Franklin Barby's eyes took on a decidedly unpleasant shine. "You want into the files. What's in it for me?"

Rett held his gaze, one part of her brain hissing like a wet cat, the other part frozen in place. "What do you mean?"

His left hand slid up her arm to her elbow. "I'm happy to help you out, Miss Smith, but I'm not supposed to let anyone into Mr. Clary's office when he's not here. I could get into trouble."

"B-but I'm here on official business, Mr. Barby." The hissing grew louder in her head. Where were her brass knuckles when she needed them? "You won't get into trouble."

Barby snorted a laugh. "You don't know Mr. Clary." He

took a step closer. "Now, what sort of agreement can we come to, Miss Smith?"

Rett yanked her hand from his and stepped back. "There is nothing I need that much to truck with the likes of you. Your boss will be hearing about this incident, Mr. Barby."

No information was worth this sort of treatment. She'd find another way.

She turned to leave, but Barby's hand clamped around her upper right arm. The hiss became a roar as Barby pulled her around.

"Hold on, Miss Smith. Let's work something ou—"

Using the momentum he'd created by turning her, Rett swung her left fist in an awkward uppercut, clipping Barby in his bony jaw. His head snapped back. He released her, staggered against the desk, hit the corner, and crashed onto the floor, out cold.

"Shit." Rett stared down at his unmoving body, barely registering that her hand now hurt like hell. She looked around the office. The only sounds in the room were the ticking of a wall clock and her rapid breathing. "Shit, shit, shit, shit, shit."

She wasn't sure what Barby was after. Money? Something else? Punching him in the face probably wasn't the best way to sort things out. Though he did put hands on her, so he got what he deserved.

She had to act fast.

She hurried to the front door, wincing when she threw the

lock. Her left hand was discolored and starting to swell. Damn it. She should have brought her brass knuckles. Dropping her satchel on the chair, she grabbed Barby under his armpits and dragged him farther behind the desk. Her hand screamed at her, and Rett bit her lip to keep herself from crying out. When she was satisfied that no one passing the window would be able to see Barby, she grabbed her satchel and dashed into Mr. Clary's office.

There were four filing cabinets in the small, neat office, all tidy, and conveniently labeled with their contents. Thank goodness for organized individuals. She scanned the precisely lettered cards in their brass frames and found the set of drawers with current and former employees. Was there anything in there to connect to Meade? To Potter?

As she yanked open the top drawer, Rett noticed the sweet aroma of recently burned tobacco. So that's what Barby was doing, stealing a smoke in the boss's office. The pipe and richer-smelling tobacco were probably more than a receptionist could afford.

Barby's pilfering was none of her concern, and she didn't have much time.

With half an ear cocked to the outside, Rett started looking through the files. From her satchel, she withdrew the list of employees Margot had discovered in her B&H archives, starting with A. J. Bonney and working her way down. None of the names matched. Same with former employees. Nothing.

Not a single name or variation on spellings were within the drawers of the B&H bakery.

Every name on her list from Margot's files represented thousands of dollars in fake hospital bills. If this Mr. Clary wasn't involved—and there was no evidence either way—that meant all the scheming came from Mrs. Gilroy and Randolph Harriman. They'd falsified the employment records and hospital receipts. Was that what Charlie Meade was blackmailing them over? No, the medical fraud occurred because Meade was going to turn them in for something else. Something Mrs. Gilroy knew had caused real harm.

Shit. She was back to square one: What had Mrs. Gilroy been talking about in her note to Margot? What had she and Randolph Harriman been doing that actually hurt people? That was serious enough to get Charlie Meade killed?

A groan and thump from the outer office caught her attention. Barby was starting to come around. She slammed the drawers shut and hurried out of Mr. Clary's office. The downed man moaned again, heels scraping the floor in an attempt to gain his footing.

Despite the great desire to give him a swift kick, Rett hurried to the door, unlocked it, and rushed out into the rain.

Twenty-Seven

When she woke to a rainy Wednesday morning, Margot wondered how Rett would fare up in Yonkers. She had itched to have Bascom bring the car around for an "impromptu" trip north. But that would undermine her desire to keep the investigation quiet. It would also undermine the trust and friendship between her and Rett.

Let the woman do her job and you do yours!

Self-admonished, she focused on the reports Hiram had sent regarding new railway lines south and west that could increase distribution, as well as advertising mock-ups for billboards, building signs, and window displays. The potential for expanding their market was everything she and her family had dreamed of: B&H products in every store across America, bringing good food to people. It was up to her to make it happen.

A soft knock on her office door brought Margot's gaze up. Amelia entered with a handful of envelopes.

"Morning post's arrived, Miss Harriman." She laid the correspondence on the desk.

"Thank you. Did you give the postman those items I needed sent?" Margot picked up the pile and flicked through the envelopes. Most were business-related, or from some charity or another. One without a postmark, her name and address in the same neat script as the envelope now locked in the desk, caught Margot's eye.

Her heart stuttered.

Another one?

"Yes, miss. Can I get you anything?"

"Please. More coffee, toast, and a soft-boiled egg, I think."

Not that the acid rising in her stomach would allow her to eat much of anything.

"I'll let Caroline know."

Margot opened the single folded paper she'd withdrawn from the envelope and audibly gasped. *Stop being nosy. Deliver the cash or you and B&H are done. Forever. Your choice. The Bronx River Gate. This is your last chance.*

"Miss Harriman, is everything all right?"

The irrational idea that Amelia could see the words from

the other side of the room had Margot jerking the page below the level of the desk. It took her a moment to steady her thoughts enough to respond.

"Just a bit of unpleasant business, Amelia. Thank you. It'll be fine."

The young woman didn't seem convinced, perhaps because Margot herself wasn't convinced, but she nodded and made her way out of the office, closing the door firmly behind her.

Margot reread the short note. "Forever"? That seemed more of a bodily threat than one of financial ruin. Part of her chided herself for being melodramatic. The other part thought of Charles Meade floating in the bay, bound, with a fatal gunshot wound.

Fifty thousand dollars. That was an obscene amount of money for an obscene reason. But until they found out what was going on and who was behind this, what could she do? What choice did she have? And if whoever was doing this was willing to threaten her, what would they do if they caught Rett Mancini snooping?

She needed to talk to Hiram Potter, then get in touch with Rett as soon as possible. This level of threat might be the only thing that would get him to come clean. It had to. They needed to work together or lose everything.

Hands trembling, Margot picked up the telephone handset

and waited for the operator to respond. "The B&H cannery office, please." She was immediately connected. The B&H receptionist answered with a cheerful greeting. "Hello, Nancy, this is Margot Harriman. Can you connect me to Mr. Potter's office, please?"

"I'm sorry, Miss Harriman, but Mr. Potter isn't here, and his secretary called in sick."

"Oh?" Margot tried to remember if Hiram had said where he'd be today. "Do you know when he'll be in?"

"No, Miss Harriman. At least not for the remainder of this morning, I'd imagine. He mentioned something about heading to Yonkers."

Margot had started moving papers and files around on her desk, searching for a note or a reminder of some sort about Hiram's meeting schedule, but stopped at the mention of the city. "Yonkers? Did he say why?"

Another "coincidence"?

"No, just muttered 'Yonkers' and 'bakery' as he left the building. Do you want me to have him call you if he returns?"

A manila folder with Giana Gilroy's name caught her eye. "Yes, please do that, Nancy. Goodbye."

"Goodbye, Miss Harriman."

She put the telephone handset in the cradle and slid the folder out from beneath other papers. Why had she pulled Mrs. Gilroy's file? She didn't recall. Maybe because the woman had been involved up to her neatly coifed graying hair. But there was still the question of what and why. The fake hospital bills weren't the end of it. Margot knew that in her gut.

She opened the folder and started reading. Nothing about Mrs. Gilroy's time with B&H stood out. She was an exemplary employee. She made a good salary and received regular wage increases. There were notes from Camille, Randolph, and Hiram about her being beneficial to the company in general or in regard to particular projects.

Everything about Mrs. Gilroy, from written appraisals to Margot's own memories, spoke of the woman's goodness and generosity. Not a single disparaging comment or incident. Ever.

But her virtuous demeanor wasn't the whole truth.

Margot felt competing emotions as she quickly read. How did a woman so greatly appreciated by and dedicated to the company get mixed up in blackmail? The only answer, really, was Margot's father. Mrs. Gilroy would have done anything for him. Anything to keep B&H running and its reputation intact. It was much easier to see Randolph going off on a harebrained idea and getting himself mucked up than to think Mrs. Gilroy dragged *him* into something untoward.

Stranger things have happened.

True. Still, between her approaching Hiram and the guilt-laden note she'd left for Margot, it was possible Mrs. Gilroy had been attempting to find a way out of the mess. As she often did, working with Randolph. But when nothing seemed to change after she spoke to Hiram, she tried to contact Margot and come clean. Increasingly, Margot was starting to think Mrs. Gilroy was less involved as an instigator and Hiram knew much more for longer than he'd admitted.

She turned to the last page of the personnel file, the one all employees had secured to the back panel of their folder for easy access: personal data, background, and whom to contact in case of an emergency. Margot glanced at the page and was about to close the file when one word caught her eye. Yonkers. Mrs. Gilroy was from Yonkers. Her cousin Letitia was listed as her next of kin. Also from Yonkers. Mrs. Gilroy had graduated from Yonkers High School. Had her cousin? Did they know Charles Meade?

I don't believe in coincidences, Rett had said.

Margot was starting to appreciate that sentiment more completely.

File in hand, she hurried out of the office, nearly bowling over Amelia.

"Oh! Excuse me, miss. I didn't—"

"My fault, Amelia. Could you please have Bascom bring the car around?" Margot headed toward the stairs. "I'll be down in five minutes. Tell him to prepare for a trip to Yonkers."

"He's not here, Miss Harriman."

Margot stopped, one foot on the first step, and turned to Amelia. "He isn't?"

"No, miss. He's gone to see his mother. She's taken ill."

"Oh, dear. I hope she recovers quickly." But how would she get to Yonkers without bringing others into her business? There was only one answer. "Can you get my goggles and motoring coat ready, please?"

Amelia looked as if Margot had asked for a herd of elephants to be brought through the foyer. "Miss?"

Margot stiffened her spine and lifted her chin, mostly for her own sake, and smiled at the young woman. "And gloves. It's a little chilly today. Best to be prepared."

Twenty-Eight

Rett retraced her path along Edwards Avenue, frequently looking back to make sure Barby wasn't following her. It wasn't until she turned the corner onto Main Street that she remembered to put up her umbrella. By then, of course, her hat and coat were dripping and her clothes felt ten pounds heavier. Heart, head, and left hand still throbbing, she forced herself to take normal strides as she fell into step with others walking toward Getty Square. As she slowed her pace, however, she started to feel chilled.

Where could she go to dry off and warm up?

Her gaze fell upon the grand sign of the Getty House. It was close and would have towels, as well as a restaurant.

As long as the price of a cup of tea didn't dip into her dollar needed to return home, she could get herself settled and back on the right track.

Rett hurried across the street, dodging puddles and carriages, and entered the hotel. She sighed with relief at the welcoming warmth, infused with the aroma of fresh flowers in tall vases and a hint of linseed oil. Quiet conversations in the lobby gave Rett a sense of security.

To the left, double French doors were open to show the linen-clad tables of a modest dining room. Several tables were occupied at this hour. She could lose herself in here, for a brief time anyway.

The silver-haired man at the desk speaking to a guest noticed her and gave her a bemused half smile. Was she supposed to be in his hotel? Rett smiled back as she veered toward the dining room, affecting her best Margot Baxter Harriman impersonation: act like you belong, wherever you are. From the corner of her eye, she noted he went back to his conversation, though she felt him tracking her. Yes, she appeared a bit bedraggled, but that was no reason to think she didn't belong in his swanky hotel. Okay, there was every reason to think she didn't belong. Until she got thrown out, however, she'd act like she was just another swell caught in the rain.

There was no maître d' on duty, so Rett found an empty table where she could keep an eye on the door. She didn't expect to see Barby pop up, shaking his fist and holding a raw steak to his jaw, but she knew to always keep entrances and exits in sight. She set her satchel and umbrella aside, within easy reach. The table was set for two. Rett took the folded napkin from the other place setting and dabbed at her damp face and hair.

"Good morning. Can I show you a menu, miss?"

The young waiter in his black and white uniform held out the large maroon folder with gilt lettering. Instinctively, Rett knew what she had in her purse would not be enough to cover any meal within those pages.

"Just tea and toast, please." He watched her sop up rainwater from her bodice. "And another napkin, if you would."

"Yes, miss."

Her shivers slowly abating, Rett took in her surroundings with a Mona Lisa smile on her face. She caught the eye of a patron or two and nodded politely, but didn't make any sort of indication she was open to conversation. Far from it. She wanted to be seen as harmless and forgettable. It didn't necessarily matter here, but blending in was good practice, like sitting in a position to watch the doors.

Granted, it was practice for a career she might not have for long.

Rett pushed aside that particular concern. She had bigger fish to fry.

The waiter strode toward her carrying his tray as if it held a choice cut filet mignon and champagne. She decided she liked this guy and would tip him as much as she could afford.

He set the teapot, cup, and a plate of perfectly toasted bread before her, followed by a silver caddy with dishes of whipped butter and strawberry jam. "Your tea and toast, miss."

"Thank you. Tell me something, um . . ."

He grinned. "David, miss."

She smiled back at him. "David. Do you know anything about Martin Scrap and Metal Fabrication?"

"Just that it's in the industrial area by the river. That seems to be where most things like that operate."

That was what she knew as well.

"And the folks who own it?"

He shrugged. "Been here for a while, so I think the same family's owned it from the start."

At least she didn't have to dig through owner records. "Are you from around here, David?"

"Yes, miss, born and raised."

That had her sit up straight. "Oh. Lovely. I'm looking for old friends who live here. The Meades?"

"Sorry, don't know any Meades."

She hadn't expected him to know Charles Meade, but it was always worth asking.

"Can I get you anything else?" David asked as someone across the dining room called for him.

"No, thanks," Rett said. "I'll finish up soon and be on my way."

"Take your time and warm up. I'll bring the bill over when you're ready." He tucked the tray under his arm and went to attend to the other patron.

Grateful, Rett didn't hurry to finish her tea and toast. She had warmed up but wasn't quite ready to trek over to Martin Scrap & Metal Fabrication. But where to find information on them and Meade? There was no Sid at city records for her to personally call on, and going to the Yonkers City Hall would mean a lot of time putting in requests. What would be the next best option?

She asked David where the public library was located and was directed several blocks south of the train station. And they'd have city directories and the Yonkers High School yearbooks available, he responded when she'd asked about that too.

"Wonderful. Thank you for all your help, David."

She could search out Charles Meade and see who his friends and acquaintances might be. The connection to this city was too strong to be ignored.

Leaving sixty-five cents on the table with the fifty cent bill—for tea and toast? She'd have to save for a dog's age to afford dinner here, let alone a holiday—Rett gathered her satchel and umbrella and left the dining room. The silver-haired man at the front desk watched her as she sauntered through the lobby. She almost turned and made a face at him but thought better of it. No need to make herself memorable.

Outside, the rain had eased to a drizzle. Rett put up her umbrella anyway; she was still damp and didn't want to get the shivers again. She flexed her left hand. There was only a hint of pain, everything moving easily. Good to know she punched well enough to not have broken anything.

Rett walked down South Broadway, along the west side of Washington Park. City Hall dominated the green space with its clock tower. The classically designed, understated yet grand library at the southwest corner of Broadway and Nepperhan Avenue was equally impressive. Trolley cars, the occasional automobile, and several horses and carriages populated the streets, creating a mix of fumes and horse manure that was reminiscent of the streets of New York City. Yes, eventually, there would be little distinction between the Bronx and Yonkers.

She climbed one of the double set of stairs to the main entrance and went in. There was an immediate sense of quiet serenity carried upon the scent of paper, leather, and furniture polish. The soles of her shoes tapped almost too loudly as she crossed the marble floor to the large, circular desk dominating the main hall. Two people occupied chairs there, an older man and a younger woman who were bent over a tome, taking notes.

The man looked up when Rett stopped opposite him. "May I help you, miss?"

He didn't whisper, but his voice was soft and clear. Rett supposed he'd been at the library for long enough to perfect the exact tone and volume necessary to maintain the subdued atmosphere.

"Yes," she said, modeling his example, "I was wondering if you had city directories and Yonkers High School yearbooks that I could look at. I'm looking for those around the classes of, oh, 1870 to 1885."

From what she'd gathered about Charles Meade, that would be about the time he was in school. She'd start there and see if she could connect Charles Meade and Giana Gilroy or anyone else in the picture. Most schemes weren't enacted among strangers. You went to people you trusted to keep their mouths shut. Though she didn't know the original scheme that Mrs. Gilroy and Randolph Harriman had gotten themselves into, Rett had the gut feeling Yonkers played a part.

The man stood, and though he was no taller than Rett, his air of authority was certain. "Of course. Miss Nelson, if you'd be so kind as to take charge of the desk, I'll show this young lady our reference section."

"Of course, Mr. Lawrence." Miss Nelson smiled briefly at Rett, then went back to her note taking.

Mr. Lawrence came around his desk. "If you'll come this way, please."

Rett followed him across the marble entry and into a side room richly paneled and lit with pendant lights. It reminded her of Sid's city records room, but much cleaner and more luxurious. This was a public library where you wouldn't be surprised to bump into royalty.

"This is a lovely building," Rett said, maintaining her hushed tone despite herself and Mr. Lawrence being the only people within the room.

Mr. Lawrence smiled with pride. "Thank you. We endeavor to keep it beautiful as well as functional. Over here, please."

He brought her to a wall of shelves with a placard reading YONKERS—LOCAL HISTORY AND EVENTS and another indicating CITY DIRECTORIES: 1800 TO PRESENT.

"These," he said, gesturing toward the historical publications, "relate to the founding of Yonkers in 1645 by Adriaen van der Donck. He was the *Jonkheer*, or 'young gentleman,' who was granted lands in this area. Yonkers is derived from that honorific."

"Fascinating," Rett said with a smile. She loved librarians and appreciated their dedication to disseminating facts, but she wasn't in the state of mind for a history lesson. "And the school yearbooks?"

Mr. Lawrence didn't seem perturbed by her redirection. He took three steps to the right and gestured again, this time at a shelf of similar sets of slender cloth-bound books. "All the yearbooks and class information for all schools that provided them, dating back to the early 1800s. Please be gentle with them. Some have not been shelved due to their delicate condition. If you find yourself in need of one, please come see me."

"Thank you very much, Mr. Lawrence. I promise to be careful."

They stared at each other for a moment. Was he expecting more from her? A handshake? A curtsey? When Rett didn't move or say anything, he gave her a slight bow and walked away.

She set her satchel and umbrella down beside one of the long tables and draped her damp coat over a chair. Water spots on Mr. Lawrence's books would be a violation of his trust. Returning to the shelves, Rett found the volumes of the Yonkers High School yearbooks for the years she thought Charles Meade might have attended. She set the books on the table and made herself as comfortable as she could get on the solid wood chairs.

"No one ever said investigation work would be a thrill a minute," she muttered, and opened the first book from 1870.

The pages were filled with drawings and long descriptions, as well as several grainy photographs of individuals and groups, buildings, and even a dog standing on its hind legs. Since she only knew the description of middle-aged Meade Margot had provided, she'd have a devil of a time finding him among the blurry-faced youths. All she could go on was the names she knew were involved in the case. If she could make a connection between them somehow, it might start to unravel a few threads.

Rett continued her perusal through the yearbooks, sometimes catching herself reading an interesting bit about a school event, or finding she had missed a page or two when she realized her mind had drifted. She sighed and backtracked, vowing to stay focused.

Her diligence paid off when the name "Martin" caught her eye. Letitia Martin, Class of 1873. The write-up noted she was the youngest in the class, taking classes along with her cousin Giana Phillips. Rett knew Giana would eventually become Mrs. John Gilroy and work for B&H.

And her cousin, Letitia Martin? Letitia . . . Letitia . . . Cousin Letitia . . . Ah! Margot's recap of Mrs. Gilroy's funeral came back to her. Cousin Letitia, who would marry Calvin Jacobs.

Was Letitia Martin Jacobs associated with Martin Scrap & Metal Fabrication? Rett would bet her eyeteeth on that, too.

That Giana Gilroy worked for B&H and Letitia Jacobs was possibly of *that* Martin family was more of a coincidence than Rett could ignore.

But where did Charles Meade fit in?

Rett got her answer on a page of several photos titled

"Family Ties." It showed group pictures naming the students who were related to one another.

One jumped out at her. Two young women and a boy of about ten. Where had she seen that trio before?

Rett stared at the photo for several seconds before it came to her: Mrs. Gilroy's house the night she and Margot had broken in.

"Holy shit."

She looked up, relieved no one else had wandered into the room to hear her. Getting tossed out of a library for profanity would be far from the worst of her offenses, actually.

She returned her attention to the image. There was a smiling Giana Phillips standing with her cousin Letitia Martin, and in front of the two, a younger boy with a round face identified as Charlie Meade. His association with the cousins was noted: Letitia Martin's stepbrother.

Was Letitia the sister Meade went to visit from time to time?

Letitia Martin Jacobs, quite possibly of Martin Scrap & Metal Fabrication, whose driver delivers sheet metal to B&H Foods and breaks into houses armed with a pistol.

Giana Phillips Gilroy, who went to work for B&H and played a role in a medical fraud scheme. Along with something else so terrible her last words were a half-written confession before she succumbed to heart failure.

Charles Meade, Letitia's stepbrother, who became a food

inspector for the State of New York extorting money from his step-cousin Giana's company.

And ended up dead.

Who was responsible for that?

The three were more than familiar, they were family.

"The family that schemes together," Rett mused aloud. She and her siblings fought from time to time, but if Letitia was somehow responsible for Charles's death, that was a whole different level of squabbling.

But from the note Mrs. Gilroy had left for Margot, it looked like she'd started to feel guilty, or was tired of paying her step-cousin, depending on her role in the whole sordid mess.

What was the extent of said mess? Medical fraud, but that wasn't all. The unfinished confession about injury or even death. From what? No one had actually been hurt as far as she and Margot could tell from the medical fraud files. Those people weren't real, so neither were the injuries. It was purely a method of shifting money out of B&H accounts without questions.

So who *had* been hurt—other than Meade—and how?

And as for Meade, why kill him now?

How did the three young people staring up from the photograph all tie into this?

More questions.

Rett sat back with a heavy sigh. "That's what you get for wanting juicier cases."

Twenty-Nine

With the handbrake engaged, Margot adjusted the choke and timing of the Cadillac, set the newfangled electric start to the proper position, then depressed the clutch. The engine came to life, settling into a grumbly purr when she adjusted the idle. So much easier and safer than having to crank the engine from the outside and risk injury. Flying cranks were hopefully a thing of the past.

"You can do this," she said to herself as she lowered her goggles, released the brake, then put the rumbling vehicle into gear. Her heart raced and, despite the damp chill in the air, sweat gathered beneath the stylish hat tied under her chin and down her spine under her long tweed coat. Not having Bascom in the passenger seat to instruct and guide her was at once terrifying and thrilling. "Slow and easy, like Bascom taught you."

Coordinating her feet and the controls, she steered the vehicle down the driveway, gravel crunching beneath the tires. After looking both ways twice, Margot pulled out onto the thankfully quiet road. She wouldn't win any races at this rate, but she had to feel comfortable operating the machine before bringing it to any sort of effective speed.

"He makes this look so easy."

Bascom certainly had been an asset over the years, and not just for driving and lessons. In fact, all her staff had been an enormous help, in ways large and small. She tried to remember that, thanking them as she could. She also needed to remember she hired people for their expertise.

Like Rett.

A tickle of guilt almost made Margot turn around. She'd promised not to interfere in the investigation. Would driving north to find Rett be intruding? What if Margot did or said something to someone that sabotaged Rett's procedure? Rett would never forgive her, and all of Margot's attempts to stay out of the public eye would be for naught.

Yet here she was, heading to Yonkers. Though she did need to let Rett know the blackmailer had escalated to dire threats, and also give her important information on the case and Mrs. Gilroy. That was justified.

But she couldn't wander around the city; she would have

to question others as to whether Rett had been by. Could Margot find her without letting others know they were connected? She'd need to speak to people without revealing her intentions. And if the opportunity presented itself, she'd want to glean what might be critical information from them. What if whomever she spoke to was the blackmailer or the killer?

Her typical manner in the boardroom was to be direct, which might cause more harm than help here. The stakes had escalated with the last anonymous note. Could she pull the wool over someone's eyes effectively enough not to tip her hand and get her or Rett killed?

Though she prided herself on her usually coolheaded demeanor, she couldn't risk getting angry or nervous and causing more problems. A cool, thoughtful head in these matters needed to prevail. Rett would know how to interrogate people without seeming to be doing so. Who else would be able to engage in that sort of conversation, perhaps give her some pointers on gently coaxing unsuspecting subjects?

Shiloh.

Margot couldn't help grinning as she remembered Shiloh and their evening together, both with Rett and CeeCee and afterward. But as much fun as it had been, she wasn't ready to reveal who she was, let alone why she'd need to gather information without people knowing.

Rett trusted Shiloh. Could Margot?

If Margot wanted to learn how to pull off something surreptitiously, she'd better trust Shiloh.

Puttering along, Margot retraced the path the taxi had taken to bring her home from Shiloh's tiny Brooklyn apartment a few days before. She wasn't much of a driver, judging by the number of times someone yelled at her, but she recalled routes and addresses well enough to get to her destination without many wrong turns.

She pulled up along the curb in front of Shiloh's building, breathing out a sigh of relief that she'd made it unscathed. A couple of women passing by gave her and the car questioning looks. There was a delivery truck down the street, though few other personal vehicles. Margot would be noted, probably, or at least her distinctive, shiny Cadillac would stand out.

Nothing to be done about it now.

Margot got out of the car, tossed her goggles onto the seat, and hurried up the steps. Was Shiloh even home? If she'd had a show last night, she might be asleep. If Margot woke the poor woman, she'd apologize.

The entryway was dimly lit, the aromas of food wafting through. Muffled voices from behind closed doors faded as she climbed the stairs.

On the second floor, she passed several apartments before stopping at the last door. Fist raised, Margot hesitated. What was making her so anxious? The thought of being seen, or of seeing Shiloh?

You are being ridiculous.

She quelled the flutter in her belly. She gave a soft but rapid knock on the scarred wood, and was soon met with Shiloh pulling the door open and blinking sleepy blue eyes.

Her eyebrows rose, more alert now. "Margot. What are you doing here? Is everything okay?"

Her blond hair was in a messy braid. The man's shirt she wore was open at the collar, loosely tucked into trousers. Black suspenders dangled by her hips, and her feet were bare.

Margot gently bit the inside of her lip, reminding herself that the purpose of her visit was to consult with Shiloh, not to ogle.

"I apologize for dropping in. Can I speak with you for a moment?"

Shiloh stepped back, the door open in invitation. Margot entered, recalling her first visit to the one-room apartment. The cozy bed in the corner by the window with its disheveled colorful covers. A sturdy overstuffed armchair with worn floral upholstery beside the bed. The clutter of framed photographs atop a chest of drawers. A hot plate and coffeepot on a table beside a small sink. Train horns in the distance. The scents of coffee, of sweat, of Shiloh.

Shiloh closed the door. "Make yourself at home."

Margot chose the upholstered chair. Shiloh sat on the bed almost directly across from her, curiosity on her handsome face.

"I need your help," Margot said, hands clasped in her lap.

"Whatever I can do, just ask."

Shiloh appeared to be sincere in her offer, and Margot's throat tightened. She had expected some sort of snappy quip, not actual concern. She considered Rett a friend, even CeeCee, and though she and Shiloh had been intimate, there had been no expectation of an emotional connection between them. Perhaps Margot had been mistaken there.

"I-I may have to do something that requires a . . . steadiness while lying."

Now the signature Shiloh smile curved her mouth. "And you came to me because I'm so good at it."

"Yes. No. I mean . . ." Why was she so flustered? "I'm sorry, I don't mean to call you a liar. You have been honest and forthright with me from the beginning, but I think your sort of skills could come in handy."

"I have all manner of skills you could enjoy."

Shiloh's wicked grin sent flames across Margot's face. How could she have been so outrageously wanton with this woman a few days ago and now unable to put two sentences together without blushing? She had to get hold of herself. "You know what I mean."

The other woman's smile softened. "I do. If you need to appear innocent while being deceptive, you've come to the right place."

Relief loosened the tension in Margot's shoulders. "Thank you. I don't have much time."

"Ah, so a down and dirty quick lesson." Shiloh rubbed her hands together. "Let's see. First of all, you need to retain the one thing you already have boatloads of."

Margot tilted her head. "I do? What?"

"Confidence. In order to convince anyone of anything, you have to project your utter confidence in what you're saying and doing, no matter how outrageous it might sound in your own ears."

Confidence in the boardroom was one thing, but this?

Noting what had to be uncertainty on Margot's face, Shiloh took her hand and gave it a gentle squeeze. "You are one of the most confident and self-assured people I know. I figured that out even in the short time we've spent together. When you see what you want, you go get it. In this case, you want information, right?"

Margot started to protest, to soften her public image, but caught herself. Shiloh was right; she did often get what she wanted when she put her mind to it.

"Second," Shiloh continued, "keep in mind that people see what they want to see or expect to see in a given scenario. Use that. When I walk down the street in these clothes, people see what they believe to be a young man, even if they're right next to me. I don't disabuse them of that because it's to my advantage. With you, they would expect to see a woman in charge, someone demanding and deserving respect. Don't disappoint them."

"Expectations and assumptions, got it," Margot said.

"Third, keep things simple. Too complicated and you may lose your place. Your audience could get suspicious enough to question and look deeper. You certainly don't want that. Also, lies close to the truth are easier to remember."

Like she had lied to Lieutenant Presley about her evening with Rett, CeeCee, and Shiloh. That hadn't been too difficult. Annoying and frustrating, but not difficult. Maybe she *could* do this.

"Confidence, expectations, simplicity." She ticked them off on her fingers. "Anything else?"

"I'm not sure what you're after, but here's something I learned from Madam Batista." When Margot shook her head to indicate she didn't recognize the name, Shiloh said, "A spirit medium. Well, that's what's on the marquee, anyway. She told me that if you know something and want to gather more information, pretend you don't know anything. If you act innocent and ask the right questions, people often offer up corrections or fill in the blanks. At the same time, if you *don't* know something, bluff and pretend you do. If you can keep the conversation general enough, the mark—I mean, the client— will slip and likely give you exactly what you need."

"Oh, I've done that before." Her conversation with Charles

Meade at his office had proceeded that way, though it hadn't been completely intentional. He had assumed she'd spoken about the blackmail agreement with Hiram when she hadn't.

Shiloh smiled. "Then you'll be fine. Magicians, grifters, and businesspeople tend to have similar skills, especially when it comes to probing for information without letting others know what they're up to."

Margot nodded, then Shiloh's words sunk in. Businesspeople? Why had she brought up businesspeople? "Do . . . do you know who I am, Shiloh?"

Rett promised she hadn't said anything to anyone, and Margot believed her. Could Shiloh have figured it out or gone "probing" on her own? Would she have read the society pages? Margot wasn't a standard fixture in the news, and she preferred it that way. She and B&H had been in the papers over the years, both as staunch supporters of the Pure Food and Drug Act and, more recently, after her father had passed away and she became the head of the company. But that had been months ago. Nothing specific had been printed since then, as far as she was aware.

Shiloh's enigmatic smile gave nothing away. "Now, Margot, being who I am, would you believe me if I told you I didn't know who you were?"

If Shiloh knew, Margot had to worry about her saying . . . what? That the president of B&H had hired an investigator? That she had broken into a dead woman's house? That she had slept with the person who'd done the actual breaking in? It wouldn't make sense for Shiloh to implicate herself, and truthfully, Margot didn't think Shiloh was the sort to turn on her or Rett.

"Perhaps you do know who I am," Margot said, "and you're just being considerate of my desire not to have you know."

That would be a sweet gesture on Shiloh's part, and another unexpected aspect of their relationship, whatever it was or turning into.

Shiloh's grin widened as she took up both of her hands and held Margot with her piercing blue eyes. "I hope you *do* believe me when I tell you none of that matters to me. It doesn't matter what your name is, or what you do for a living. I consider myself a decent judge of character, whatever that character may be. What matters to me is that I think you're a good person. I enjoy spending time with you and want to do it more often."

Margot swallowed the lump that formed in her throat. For one of the few times in her life, if she were to believe Shiloh—and she truly wanted to—here was someone not interested in knowing her for her name or her position or her connections. She wanted to know Margot for being Margot.

"I feel the same about you, Shiloh."

"And you know more about me than I do about you, so I take that as a compliment." She winked and Margot laughed.

"But honestly, Margot, I like you and I hope we can be friends, even if I know who you are."

Margot nodded and gently squeezed the other woman's hands. "I'd like that too."

"Good." Shiloh pressed her lips against Margot's knuckles, her intense gaze never wavering. "Can you stay for a bit?"

Heat shimmered through Margot, along with a quiver low in her belly reminiscent of their previous time together. She smiled sadly, reluctant to douse those feelings. But doused they must be. For now. "I wish I could, but I have to head out. Another time, I promise. Can you tell me the quickest way to get to Yonkers?"

Margot navigated out of Shiloh's neighborhood, over the Williamsburg Bridge spanning the East River, and eventually to roads north through Manhattan. She drove somewhat faster, though she was still getting a feel for the vehicle and what it could do.

With the suggestions Shiloh provided and a map opened on the passenger seat, she didn't find it to be a difficult drive. The occasional vehicle passed her, kicking up flecks of mud with the rain that made her grateful for her windscreen and her goggles, even with the top up.

Once she crossed the bridge, however, the busy streets, pedestrians, trolley cars, and other vehicles made her tense. Margot drove even more slowly in these areas, much to the consternation of experienced drivers who had no qualms about yelling for her to hurry the hell up. Mostly she ignored them, used to men challenging her methods, though with less vocalized profanity. She was, as always, determined to get where she was going in one piece.

Traffic thinned as she passed through Harlem and into the Bronx, where she was able to pick up speed with more confidence. After the better part of an hour, she reached the city of Yonkers.

Margot pulled over on South Broadway, a main road leading to Getty Square, to catch her breath and recheck her map. She wanted to go to the B&H Bakery first, since that was where Rett was headed. A glance at her pendant watch told her it was after eleven. Rett had said she'd be in Yonkers by ten. Would she stick to her schedule? If she had already visited the bakery, how would Margot find her?

"Sitting on the side of the road certainly won't accomplish anything," she muttered to herself, and put the Cadillac into gear with only a small grind of metal on metal.

The boulevard grew increasingly busy as she continued north, but rather than going into the heart of the city at Getty Square, she veered to the right, down Main Street. When Bascom drove, she was free to take in the shops and the people and vehicles, but concentrating on who was coming alongside her, or which truck or carriage was going to cross in front of her, took all of Margot's mental focus. Luckily, her next turn onto Nepperhan Avenue was easy enough, as it was a wide road. But trying to find the side street on the left took her more than one attempt.

Finally, she managed to turn down Edwards Avenue, upsetting a man with a wheelbarrow coming out of an alley.

"Sorry!" she yelled back to him, shooting into the dirt lot in front of the B&H Bakery.

Pushing down on the clutch and the brake, Margot caused the Cadillac to slide a short distance in the mud before coming to a stop near the door. She shifted into neutral, set the brake, adjusted the choke, and flipped the operating switch from battery to off. The engine rumbled then shut down. She then set the levers for the throttle and idle in preparation for the next time she started the vehicle, as Bascom taught her.

Margot took a moment to collect herself, removing her goggles and blotting away perspiration with her handkerchief. Truth be told, she was quite pleased with herself. She could drive her own vehicle. Not that she was ready to give up Bascom; he was vital to her as a friend as well as a driver.

Still, simply knowing she was capable kept her smiling as she stepped down from the car and headed to the door. Margot entered the bakery office, something she'd done many times.

Confidence, expectations, simplicity.

Mr. Barby was at his desk, as he often was on her visits. Mr. Clary's office door was closed.

"May I help—Oh! Good morning, Miss Harriman." Barby stood and gave a slight bow, his hand gently rubbing his jaw. "We weren't expecting you today."

Margot smiled benignly. Barby wasn't a bad sort, though he tended to be simultaneously obsequious and condescending. "Good morning. I decided to go for a little drive and found myself headed north. Thought I'd drop in."

"It *is* your facility, Miss Harriman." His smile was as forced as her own. "Is your driver outside? I have tea water heating if the two of you would like to warm up."

"I drove myself," Margot said, and nearly laughed at the startled look on his face. "I'll pass on the tea, thank you. How are things here? Any excitement?"

She hoped she didn't sound too anxious.

Barby gave a bark of a laugh. "No. No, ma'am."

"Is Mr. Clary in? I wanted to talk to him about the visit from the state clerk."

His eyes widened. "How'd you know about that?"

Margot gave him another smile, this one hopefully expressing the gentle reproach—and confidence—she meant when she said, "Truly, Mr. Barby? As you just said, this is *my* facility." Expectations. "The state let us know they'd be sending someone up today to rectify some paperwork. Have they not arrived yet?"

Simplicity. The cover Rett was supposed to use to gain

access to the files may have been somewhat elaborate, but the story was not.

"Yes. She did." Barby's gaze dropped to his desk. "She left. Because Mr. Clary wasn't in. To help her. Said she'd return tomorrow."

"She?" Margot pretended to be surprised because *of course* having a woman on staff at the state's Factory Investigating Committee office in a field position would be a shock. "That's unusual."

But Rett saying she'd return tomorrow? They hadn't considered her needing to return.

Something wasn't right.

"Quite." Barby didn't hide his lack of enthusiasm for Rett's visit, though whether it was due to Rett herself or that a woman was working for the state, it was difficult to tell. "But she's gone now."

"Yes, I can see that." Margot watched him for a moment. "How about Mr. Potter? Has he stopped in today?"

Barby ran his palm along his jaw, frowning. "No. Was he supposed to?"

That was what Nancy had told her, but she couldn't be sure what Hiram was up to anymore.

"He said he might be in the neighborhood." Margot noted that Mr. Barby didn't seem particularly pleased at the idea of two B&H higher-ups dropping in for a visit. In fact, he looked rather miserable. Was that a bruise? "What happened to your jaw, Mr. Barby?"

He stopped rubbing his face. "Toothache."

Images of Rett with her brass knuckles flashed through her head. Surely she hadn't assaulted her employee. At least not without a good reason.

"Perhaps you should get that looked at." Barby mumbled something that Margot chose to ignore. "Did the woman from the state say where she was headed?"

"No." He seemed confused. "Was she supposed to meet with you, too, Miss Harriman?"

"No, not officially. There's something coming up in the regulations I wish to speak to someone about. I thought while she was here in town I'd chat with her. How long ago did she leave? Maybe I'll catch her somewhere close."

Barby looked at the clock on the wall. "She, um, she left about half an hour ago."

Damn it. Rett could be anywhere in the city by now if she'd caught a streetcar or trolley. Would she have gone somewhere other than Martin's? The metalwork facility and the bakery were the only two locations they'd discussed, but if Rett thought of something else to investigate, she'd go for it.

"And all is well, Mr. Barby? No problems or injuries to report? Other than your tooth, I mean."

His cheeks reddened. "No, Miss Harriman. The woman

was asking about that as well. She was looking for medical claims and safety issues."

Margot feigned curiosity. "Did she? So nice they're concerned about such things. Did you have anything to tell her?"

"Well, no." Barby appeared bemused. "I don't have any memory of any injuries here that would have required a claim like that. And with Mr. Clary out, the employee files aren't accessible."

No injuries of significance? Barby would have assisted with the paperwork, so he would be the one to know. Was he lying? Or did that confirm no one other than Mrs. Gilroy and her father had been involved in fraud? That was a relief, at least.

"Too bad I missed her. I could have shown her the files," Margot said.

Barby's eye twitched. "But Mr. Clary's door is locked."

"You don't have a spare key?"

"N-no, ma'am."

"How unfortunate. We should remedy that."

"If you wish, Miss Harriman."

"Good thing I have a copy on my key set." She patted her reticule and almost laughed out loud when she saw him pale. "I'll be back if I find the young woman. Good morning, Mr. Barby. Please get that tooth looked at."

Margot turned around and headed for the door before Barby could see her smiling.

"Yes, Miss Harriman. Good morning."

She returned to the car and sat in the driver's seat. Rain pattered off the soft roof, occasionally blowing in through the gap between the roof and windscreen.

Where could Rett be? What else was in Yonkers that would interest the investigator? She didn't know about Giana Gilroy having grown up here, but she knew about Charles Meade and Martin Scrap & Metal Fabrication. If she were Rett, that's where she'd go next.

Margot set her goggles over her eyes. "The metalworks it is."

Thirty

Rain fell hard and steady as Margot made her way west through Getty Square. Martin Scrap & Metal Fabrication occupied a section of the industrial area beside the Hudson River. She had never been, but checking a Yonkers directory that Mr. Barby had on hand gave her the information she needed. Poor Mr. Barby looked even more miserable with his sore jaw when she had dashed back in to ask if he had the directory, and she hoped he'd get it looked at sooner rather than later.

According to her map, she needed to take North Broadway to Lamartine Avenue, turn right on Ravine Avenue, then left on Point Street. Martin Scrap & Metal Fabrication should be across the railroad tracks, near the Habirshaw Wire Company.

Taking Broadway north allowed her to avoid trolley, streetcar, and most pedestrian traffic, though there were more vehicles to watch for in the heart of the city. Eventually, the density of dwellings and businesses lessened as she passed a school and a church. There was also a reduction in the number of vehicles on the road, and Margot was able to relax a little as she continued to Lamartine, Ravine, and Point Street. There ahead of her was the wire company and the metalworks.

"Excellent," she said as she drew to a stop before the building with barely a skid in the mud. A metal door with the word OFFICE on it was set in the massive brick wall. The name of the company had been painted above the door in three-foot tall letters. Two tarp-covered automobiles sat in the lot, older models from what she could see of them.

Margot removed her goggles, straightened her hat, and got out. The bite of hot metal tinged the air, carried on the black smoke that wafted out of three brick chimneys. She walked around the side of the building. A tall wooden fence enclosing a large lot extended all the way to the river fifty yards away. She peeked through a gap between the gate and the fence post. Small mountains of scrap metal filled the lot, while the rumble of machinery and the crashing of metal on metal created a near-deafening cacophony even from a distance. Men in grimy work clothes wearing leather gloves moved in and out of a bay door.

Several trucks with the MARTIN SCRAP & METAL FABRICATION sign on their sides were parked facing the gate.

Margot returned to the front door, turned the knob, and went in. The Martin's office was tiny but tidy, with just a desk, a chair, and a telephone. Two interior doors led out of the room, both closed. The rumble of machinery could be heard through one door and felt through the soles of her shoes. Margot wasn't sure what exactly went on at a metalworks, other than making the sheets of tin and steel necessary for canning. Whatever it was, it was loud and hot.

She opened the collar of her coat and fluttered the fabric. It was considerably warmer in the office than she'd expected on a damp spring day.

No one appeared at the sound of the heavy outer door shutting. Should she wait for someone to arrive?

Just as Margot was about to call out, a young blonde in an emerald green dress came in through the door that didn't seem to have machinery running behind it. She was focused on the paper in her hand and didn't see Margot at first. When she looked up, her hand went to her chest, as if to keep her shocked heart in. But she smiled almost immediately.

"Hello! I'm sorry, I didn't expect anyone to be here. We don't get many visitors, and you're our second today. Metalworks isn't exactly a thing most people take a casual or daily interest in, is it? Not like a grocer's or the post office or a shoe store or something. How do you do? I'm Jenny."

She stuck out her right hand.

Margot smiled at the vivacious woman and shook her hand. "How do you do? I'm Margot Harriman. My company has an account with you for sheet tin and steel. I want to make sure we are all up-to-date on our payment and order schedule."

All these details had already been taken care of a month ago by Hiram and others, but it was the only reason Margot could come up with for being there.

Jenny bit her lower lip. "I'm not able to access account information like that, Mrs. Harriman. You'd need to talk to Mrs. Jacobs."

"It's Miss Harriman." But the name she mentioned caught Margot's attention. "Mrs. Jacobs? Letitia Jacobs?"

Jenny smiled. "Yes, that's right. She and her husband are the new owners. Well, I suppose they've always been owners, in a sense, since she's a Martin. But they started running things after Mr. Martin, her father, passed away. God rest his soul."

The connection between Giana Gilroy and Martin Scrap & Metal Fabrication made sense now. Contracting goods and services between companies where families worked wasn't terrible or unusual as far as the ethics of nepotism went, as long as no one was being given preferential treatment. Or excessively profiting from the arrangement. But considering the current situation, something made the back of Margot's neck sweat.

"Mr. J. runs the shop, and Mrs. J. takes care of the books. Hardly anyone is allowed to look at them besides her."

I bet, Margot thought. "Is Mrs. Jacobs available?"

Jenny gestured toward the door from which she had entered. "She's in the back. Let me go ask her if she can be disturbed." She turned back to the door, knocked a couple of times, and opened it. "Huh. She's not there." Jenny shut the door and faced Margot. "There's a door that leads to the shop. She may have gone to see about something out there. I'm not supposed to go out on the shop floor. Too dangerous. Would you like to wait? I can get another chair."

Margot considered it. "Thank you, but that won't be necessary. I'll come back another time."

"All right." Jenny smiled brightly. "I'll let her know you came by."

Margot almost told her not to bother, but that might seem like an odd request. Businesspeople usually wanted to know others were trying to make contact. "That would be fine. Good afternoon, Jenny."

"Good afternoon, Miss Harriman."

Just as her hand touched the knob, something else pinged in her brain, and Margot turned around. "Jenny, you said you had another visitor here today. Was it a young woman, by chance?"

"No," Jenny said, shaking her head. "An older gentleman. Very dapper and polite. Fussed with his hanky like my grandpa used to. He wanted to see Mrs. Jacobs as well."

Hiram. It had to be.

"Is he still here?"

"No. His car was gone when I got back from an errand for Mrs. J. She had to have a letter posted right away. Couldn't wait until the postman came this afternoon." Jenny smiled and shrugged at the eccentricities of her employer.

"I see. Thank you. Good day."

Margot left the office, returning to her car while silently cursing. Aside from being Mrs. Gilroy's cousin and cousin-in-law, how did Letitia and Calvin Jacobs fit into this? Had they hired their own truck driver to search Mrs. Gilroy's home? There was no need if they were going there the following day. That meant one of them probably wasn't aware of what was going on and needed to keep their spouse in the dark. Did they have their driver kill Charles Meade? If so, why? And what had Hiram been doing here?

She felt a tightening of her gut. Was Hiram involved in the scheme and murder? There was no other reason for him to visit Martin's.

Margot started her vehicle. Now that it was warm, the engine fired right up, growling quietly like a tiger that wasn't sure if it should be irritated or pleased with your attention.

Had Letitia or Calvin Jacobs sent the blackmail note demanding money be left at the Bronx Zoo? Had they sent the note threatening Margot's life? Had Hiram, to throw her off?

That thought was too much to consider, but consider it she must.

Mrs. Gilroy said people were being hurt. But the medical fraud was the exact *opposite* of that. No one was physically injured there. So what, then? And what did the Jacobses and Martin Scrap & Metal Fabrication have to do with it? What would Hiram need to see them about?

Margot released the handbrake and swung the Cadillac around. She bumped over the railroad tracks, heading east on Point Street. There hadn't been much pedestrian traffic this close to the industrial area when she drove in, and the lone figure beneath the black umbrella caught her eye.

Is that . . . ?

Margot pressed the brake and the clutch to stop, sliding in the mud and just managing to get the shifter into neutral before she stalled the engine.

"Rett?" she called out.

Thirty-One

Rett lifted her head at the sound of her name. She knew no one in Yonkers. But she did recognize the maroon Cadillac stopped in front of her.

"Margot? What are you doing here? Is everything all right? Where's Bascom?"

"Everything's . . . Well, it is what it is. Get in."

Rett hurried around to the passenger side. The interior of the car was only slightly warmer than the rain. She shook water off her umbrella after folding it and looked around for somewhere to deposit the dripping accessory.

"Toss it in the back," Margot said, and put the vehicle into gear. "I figured you'd be headed here at some point."

A MURDEROUS BUSINESS

"What are *you* doing here, Margot?" Rett asked again, barely managing to keep her irritation in check. "I thought we agreed you'd stay out of the actual investigation."

She had believed Margot when she said she'd let Rett handle things. Was the woman incapable of relinquishing the reins to others? Rett had always thought a good businessperson knew when to delegate. If Margot couldn't step back long enough to let Rett do her job, Rett had to consider dropping her case. That was not something she wanted to do for a number of reasons.

"I know, and I apologize," Margot said, sounding legitimately sorry. "But another threatening note arrived, and I was worried about you. Also, I came across something I wanted to share with you as soon as possible."

"Another note?" Rett's heart rate kicked up. "What does it say?"

Margot motioned toward her purse while she steered around a suspiciously deep-looking puddle. "In there."

Rett withdrew the envelope from Margot's bag and removed the single sheet. Same handwriting, from what she recalled of the first. Shorter sentences. To the point. Someone was getting nervous. Nervous people often became dangerous people. Charles Meade might have learned that the hard way.

"Holy Hannah, Margot."

"That's mostly why I came," she said, turning onto another street a little too fast. Rett braced her hand against the dashboard. "Sorry. That and something niggling about Giana Gilroy and Letitia Jacobs."

"They went to school here together," Rett said. "Not a surprise as they're family."

"So you know Letitia's maiden name was Martin."

Rett nodded. "Yeah, I found a yearbook at the library." She glanced at Margot. "But there's something else. Charles Meade was Letitia's stepbrother."

"What?" Margot startled so hard, she swerved and nearly ran them into an oncoming car. Rett's heart rate jumped painfully. "They're *all* related?"

"Yep." Rett kept her hands braced on the seat and door, watching for dangers ahead. "We have that connection made."

Margot turned toward Main Street. "Hiram came up here today. I have no idea why. He told the receptionist at the cannery he was going to the bakery."

"Barby didn't say anything about that, though he might not to the likes of me."

Margot shook her head. "He didn't mention Hiram to me either, but it seems that Hiram may have gone to Martin's."

"Martin's? Why?" There was no reason Rett could conjure for the B&H manager to visit them. Or why he wouldn't tell anyone that he was going to visit them. Unless he didn't want others to know. "This isn't good, Margot."

The older woman squinted slightly as she concentrated on the road. "I know. Hiram said Mrs. Gilroy had told him everything, which could have involved Martin's somehow. But I can't see him being involved in murder."

Rett held her tongue. Couldn't see it or didn't want to see it? Despite her demand for the truth, Margot might not be ready for the brutal reality of it.

"I know, I know," she said as if reading Rett's mind. She glanced across the space of the car, a wry, sad smile curving her mouth. "I said I wanted the truth. Whatever it is. I just can't quite believe it. But if that's what it is, that's what it is."

Rett could only nod. This was the hardest part of the job, the client learning the truth of their suspicions. Whether it was a spouse wondering if their partner was cheating on them, or a businesswoman worrying if a longtime family friend might be involved in murder and blackmailing her and her company, learning the truth was never easy.

"What's the next step?" Margot asked. The area they drove through became increasingly populated; they were back in the heart of Yonkers.

"With what you've just said," Rett answered, "it might be a good idea to figure out why Hiram Potter went to Martin Scrap and Metal Fabrication."

Margot glanced at her, bemused. "We can't seem to find Hiram, and returning to Martin's to let Letitia know we're poking around can't be a good thing."

"Agreed." Rett sat back and rubbed her arms. Her shivering hadn't abated yet. "We'll go back later and find your account files when we don't have to worry about Letitia or anyone else."

Her attention back to the road, Margot got the gist of what Rett was saying. "Ah. Understood. We'll have to wait until the workers have left for the day. After dark."

"Nightfall won't come for a few hours yet. We can lie low until then."

"And warm you up some. Let's go to the Getty. Lunch and a dry room are on me."

"Good." Rett laughed. "Because they certainly aren't expenses I can cover."

Thirty-Two

The room Margot had acquired at the Getty was perhaps the most luxurious Rett had ever been in. A shame they would only be there for the afternoon. Feather pillows, down comforters, even heated towel racks in the private bathroom! Who had heated towel racks? Maybe they were a staple for the likes of Margot Baxter Harriman, but such a thing was well beyond anything Loretta Mancini had encountered. One of these days she'd scrape enough money together to bring CeeCee here for a holiday. Well, for a night at least.

She and Margot had been able to dry off, warm up, eat, and even pretend to rest while they waited for nightfall. Now they sat in the Cadillac, a block away from Martin Scrap &

Metal Fabrication, making sure no one was coming or going as the rain continued to plop down.

"Looks pretty quiet," Margot said as she scanned the street.

"It does." Rett shook her head slightly. "I still don't like the idea of you being out here."

"I know, but it's too much ground for one person to cover."

She sighed in resignation. "I suppose. Just don't do anything to get yourself into a pickle."

Margot quirked an eyebrow. "Like clobber a man from behind?"

"Only if you have to."

Margot smiled at her, but her expression had a hint of tension. As much as she was game for involvement, Margot wasn't used to such action. But Rett knew she wouldn't back away either.

"Stay close. We'll go around to the side gate. More concealed than at the front door." Rett checked her pockets: picks, flashlight, no brass knuckles. Damn it. "Ready?"

Margot pulled the collar of her coat up and adjusted her hat. "Ready."

They got out of the Cadillac and walked with a casual air, as if they had every right to be there, even at night. Nervous-looking people drew attention, Albert always told her. He'd caught plenty of petty criminals while walking his beat because they'd seemed "off" or twitchy.

They veered to the left side of the building, feet crunching on gravel. Rett noted windows along the otherwise solid brick wall. That must be where the offices were. The rest of the front wall was interrupted by only a single door. As they drew closer, the sound and smell of the river grew stronger, along with the expected metallic tinge in the air. There was also a smokiness that made sense if a smelter ran for hours on end.

The truck-sized wooden gate was closed, a thick chain padlocked around the metal frames. Tire tracks disappeared under the gate, softening in the muck. Rett peered through the gap. No one seemed to be about.

She took her pick set out of her pocket. From the other, she withdrew the flashlight and handed it to Margot. As the food company president and heiress found the switch and kept the light trained low, Rett wondered if she had ever expected herself to be skulking about a locked building at night, preparing to break in. Breaking and entering weren't part of any finishing school curriculum. It wasn't in any Catholic school curriculum either, though she was sure Sister Benedictus wouldn't be terribly surprised to see where Rett was at the moment.

Rett crouched down and unrolled the cloth case along her thigh. She chose the tension wrench and a couple of picks. "Hold the light close," she whispered.

Margot did as asked. "Have you been practicing?"

Rett gave an amused grunt. "You sound like Shiloh. Yes, I have."

She maneuvered the picks, feeling for give or resistance. After a minute and a couple of muttered curses, the telltale feel of tumblers moving and a quiet snick marked her success. The hasp dropped away from the lock body with a gentle tug.

Smiling, Rett returned her tools to the case and put them away.

"Well done." Margot kept the light trained low while Rett removed the lock from the chain and carefully slid the chain from the frame.

They opened the gate only wide enough to slip through. Rett draped the chain around the frame and hooked the lock hasp through a couple of the links. It would be obvious on close inspection that something was amiss, but hopefully no one would be coming that close.

The Martin's yard was pitch-black, except for a single light over each of the three person-sized doors. There were several larger bay doors farther along the wall.

Margot swept the beam of light across the ground. It hit a nearby pile of debris, dark and twisted junk. Old stoves, lengths of pipe, unidentifiable dull or blackened metal that stretched beyond the limits of the flashlight.

"Amazing to think this is what your cans are made of," Rett said. She couldn't disguise the distaste in her words. Sure, she knew the metal was melted down and the impurities burned out, but looking at the puddles beneath the scrap, there were questionable glints and swirls of leaking chemicals.

"The melting process does the job," Margot said. "Though how they assure the composition of the metal sheets is more of a challenge."

"What do you mean? Don't you want pure metals?" Sister Mary Michael's chemistry lessons lingered at the back of Rett's brain.

"Not necessarily." Margot moved the light around the pile of junk. "Alloys are useful. They can be stronger and lighter than pure metals, and cheaper too. But you can't use any old metals or alloys. It's not safe."

Something in the way she ended the sentence caught Rett's attention.

"Margot?"

Margot swung the light around, training it on Rett's chest. "That's it, Rett. People getting sick. It's been in the papers. But not from the food in the cans, it's from the metal in the cans. Lead or arsenic or both. Something in the *cans* making people sick."

Rett looked out onto the shadowed yard. How much metal was there? And what sort?

Mrs. Gilroy's note about people falling ill and dying, the involvement of Martin Scrap & Metal Fabrication, what Meade was holding over B&H. It all came together in a swirling cloud that coalesced into understanding.

"That's what's happening," Rett said. "The metal you're being sold isn't safe."

Margot paled in the poor light. "We were supposed to be guaranteed food-quality sheet metal."

"I bet it costs a pretty penny, too," Rett said. Margot nodded. "And I'd also bet Martin's is charging you for that fancy expensive, safe metal but sending cheaper, dangerous stuff. That would make them a nice profit."

Switching out products and pocketing the difference was one of the oldest grifts in the book. But in this case, the use of that lesser product was hurting people. Letitia and Calvin Jacobs's company supplied the tainted metal. Mrs. Gilroy knew about it. Randolph Harriman knew about it. Charles Meade had used that information to blackmail B&H. Hiram Potter eventually knew everything as well.

And Margot would be left holding the bag.

Distant voices calling out, doors rattling shut, water flowing along the banks of the Hudson—the sounds of the Yonkers riverside at night surrounded them as the weight of events pressed on Margot's shoulders.

"How long has it been going on?" Margot asked, almost to herself. "And how do we prove it?"

"We need to get inside the office and find some hard evidence. There has to be something," Rett said. "We can take metal samples here and at your cannery."

"An independent laboratory can test the samples." Margot started toward the lit door at the rear of the building. "If we can prove that Martin's knew they were selling us dangerous material—"

Rett grabbed her arm, stopping her. "Margot, wait. You're putting yourself and B&H in the line of fire."

Margot stared at her. When she spoke, her voice cracked. "I know."

Rett's heart broke for her. The people she trusted most had betrayed her company, had put innocent customers in danger, and here she was ready to prove their wrongdoing. She'd risk everything, and suffer because of it, but she was more concerned with stopping the crimes than her own welfare.

"I told you I wanted to know the truth, no matter what it was," Margot said, grief filling her eyes but determination setting her jaw. "I'm sticking by that, Rett. I know it's going to be bad for B&H, for me, but I wouldn't be able to live with myself otherwise. You'll help me save my company if we can, won't you?"

Rett squeezed her arm. "Of course. Come on."

They strode over to the door and Rett took out her picks again. This lock appeared to be more formidable.

"This one might take a bit," she said, inserting the slender tools and testing resistance.

Margot said nothing. She held the light steady. Rett could only imagine what was going through her head.

Twisting the tension wrench and a pick, Rett felt the metal tool bend. "Shit."

She eased off and tried to withdraw the pick. It didn't move. "Damn it."

"What now?" Margot asked, a hint of concern in her voice.

"Hang on." Rett chose a thinner pick. "Let me try something."

She maneuvered the new pick alongside the one that had bent. Carefully, she wiggled them both and the tension wrench. If the new pick wasn't able to support the compromised tool . . . She felt the tumbler give as the lock clicked. "Aha!"

"Brilliant," Margot said.

Rett turned the knob, and they entered the office. With no windows to reveal them, Rett turned the switch on a desk lamp. The light showed two other doors, one leading to the reception area Margot had mentioned, the other to the fabrication plant. The office was tidy with a desk, chairs, shelves of ledgers and books, and the distinct odor of burnt metal.

"Letitia's office," Margot whispered.

"There has to be something in here we can use. You check the desk." Rett gestured to one of the shelves. "I'll see what's in these ledgers."

Rett pulled one of the large books off the shelf. Account records, orders going back a few years, depending on the customer. Nothing she could see as untoward or illegal.

"Find anything?" she asked.

"Nothing obvious," Margot replied, "but I'd expect any evidence to be hidden, masked in some way."

"Right. Or a second set of books. See if there's any sort of false bottoms on drawers or hidden panels."

Margot scoffed. "You read too many dime store novels."

"You'd be surprised how many criminals read dime store novels. Or how many write them."

The other woman chuckled softly, but Rett noticed she was feeling along the bottoms of drawers and knocking on the side of the desk.

"One thing doesn't make sense," Margot said.

"What's that?" The ledger with B&H account information didn't look suspect. Rett was considering taking the pages out of it to compare with Margot's files.

"Why kill Charles Meade?"

Rett started to offer her opinion on that when the door leading to the reception area flew open, slamming against the wall. Both Rett and Margot jumped. Rett's heart thundered, her hand dropping into her empty pocket. *Shit, shit, shit.* No brass knuckles.

In the doorway, an older woman in a long wool coat, her graying black hair in a severe bun, held a gun. The deadly black hole was pointed right at Margot's chest. She kept the door open with one hand as she scowled at them.

"Because he got greedy," she said, storm gray eyes jumping between Rett and Margot. "Greedy and too big for his britches."

Thirty-Three

"Letitia," Margot said with a steadier voice than she'd expected, all things considered. "You don't have to do this."

"He horned in on your deal, didn't he?" Rett made an assumption Margot hadn't entertained. "Started pushing for more money than he deserved."

Letitia swung the gun toward Rett, her face red. Margot's heart stuttered. "Exactly. I told him he shouldn't bug Giana for more money, but did he listen to me? No. Then after Randolph died, Giana got nervous and told Potter about Charlie. He was blowing the whole damn thing because he wanted more. He always wanted more."

"You sold us tainted metal." Margot struggled to keep the

anger out of her voice to avoid agitating the woman into any rash actions. She wanted to defend herself and Rett, but had nothing to counter Letitia's gun. Not even a ceramic pitcher. "People got sick."

Letitia shrugged. "People get sick all the time."

"How did you get Mrs. Gilroy to agree to all this?" Rett asked.

Margot still had a hard time seeing sweet Mrs. Gilroy as a criminal, let alone a criminal mastermind, but Rett didn't have the burden of familiarity.

The bark of laughter that came from Letitia told her she was not going to like the response. "Gia came to *me* with the idea. She and Randolph were looking to reduce costs so the company could make more competitive bids on bulk contracts. Wanted a less expensive material. I gave them an option, they took it." Her gaze narrowed at Margot. "You didn't know? Silly girl."

Margot felt the blood drain from her face. She had suspected, of course, but actually hearing what her father and Mrs. Gilroy had done from someone else hit harder than her speculation. She had to start letting go of assumptions about people she thought she knew. "No, I didn't know."

"Well, now you do. Not that it matters." Letitia clucked her tongue as if disappointed. "You should have just paid the fifty grand."

The blackmail payment to be left at the Bronx Zoo.

"You sent the notes," Margot said. "But why threaten to expose B&H when your scheme would have been revealed as well? We all would have suffered."

"I assure you, Miss Harriman, I was prepared for the consequences of exposure. If you didn't pay, and I was pretty sure you would to save your precious name, I have enough stashed away to disappear and leave Cal wondering what hit him."

Poor Calvin Jacobs. He had no idea who he'd married.

Letitia's expression hardened. She gestured toward Rett with the gun. "Now, open the other door, slowly. Funny business gets you shot."

Margot had the sick feeling they were going to be shot either way. Delaying that as long as possible would be to their distinct advantage.

She and Rett exchanged looks. Something in the investigator's eyes told Margot she had a plan. Whatever that might be, Margot had no idea. She'd have to be ready for anything.

Rett moved toward the door that led into the work area. She turned the knob and pushed the door open, but she didn't go through. Residual heat and the smell of hot metal from the smelter wafted out of the dimly lit, high-ceiling room. Racks and shelves blocked the view of the vast space.

"Move," Letitia said, pointing with the gun again.

Rett motioned for Margot to go first, putting herself in the path of potential bullets.

"Rett . . ." That she would risk her own safety threatened to overwhelm Margot. Her hands grew cold, and her stomach quivered.

"Just go ahead," Rett said. "Please."

Trusting Rett, Margot walked through the open doorway. Rett followed close behind her. Just as Rett seemed to clear the opening, Margot felt a shove between her shoulder blades strong enough to send her stumbling. She managed to keep her feet, barely.

"Go!" Rett shouted, moving behind her.

A gunshot cracked as the door slammed.

"Run," Rett yelled. "Get out! Don't worry about me!"

Margot glanced over her shoulder. Rett had her back against the metal door. On the other side, Letitia Jacobs fired another shot.

"Go!" Rett waved Margot to the left while she dashed to the right, around tall racks of stacked sheet metal.

Margot ran.

She skirted the opposite corner of the shelving, along the closed bay doors that led to the scrap yard. Farther along, she saw a regular-sized door and ran toward it.

Behind her, the door to Letitia's office slammed open, crashing into the wall.

"Bitch!" echoed across the ceiling.

Crack!

Something whizzed past Margot's ear. The cement wall

beside her threw up bits of rock. Instinctively, Margot ducked her head and closed her eyes against damage. A piece flew into her cheek, stinging the skin below her left eye.

Another shot ricocheted off the door jamb.

Stopping to try to open the door, to get to safety, was too risky.

Margot darted down the aisle between two sets of racks and crouched down. Through the gaps in the shelves, she saw another huge workroom beyond the racks. Would that be a way out? Could she reach it before Letitia caught up with her?

A shadow darted past the other side of the shelves. Rett? Letitia? She didn't dare call out.

Margot steadied her breathing, taking slow, deep breaths through her mouth. Where was Letitia? Where was Rett?

Careful to expose as little of herself as possible, she peered out into the aisle between racks. No one. Margot darted across the gap to the narrow space between the next set of shelves. If Letitia caught her in the more restrictive space, she was done. But nothing seemed to be moving.

There was a third row of shelves before the room opened again to the next area. Margot saw several machines she didn't recognize. The nearest had metal rollers over a bulky, boxy body. Farther on, another wide but low-profile machine. Beyond that, three low, sooty, brick stacks were closer to the far wall. Atop the stacks were crucibles to melt the junk metal.

Overhead, chains, pulleys, hooks, and gears crisscrossed the ceiling.

Metal clattered against metal somewhere nearby.

Margot bit her lips to keep from making any sound. She needed a weapon. The shelves she stood among held stacks of ingots of dull metal. Too big and heavy to be effective. Surely there were some sort of tools or scrap metal around.

This side was the finished product, sheets and sheets of metal, all neat and organized. She looked across to the other half of the processing area. That part of the operation might hold the most potential for a handy weapon. She just had to get there without being shot.

Standing around waiting to be found wasn't going to do anything useful. At the very least, she could be a moving target.

Margot ignored the sick feeling in her stomach and bolted toward the corner of the first hulk of machinery. There was a door on that wall somewhere, another chance to get away.

Footsteps scrambled behind her. Margot ran in a half crouch, making herself as small as she could.

"Damn it!"

Was that Rett?

Something crashed. Another shot ricocheted off metal. A woman cried out.

"Rett!"

Nothing.

Margot resisted the urge to turn back, to see if Rett needed help. She had said to run. One of them had to make it to safety and alert the authorities. But to leave Rett behind? That didn't sit right either.

There! The door leading outside, not far from one of the three smokestacks above a pit that glowed a dull orange and gray. The heat hit her as she reached the door. If it was this warm when the fire was banked, she could imagine how blistering it was when there was active melting of metal going on.

Near the door stood a rack with various-sized shovels, metal rakes, and long metal poles with charred ends. Not as easy to handle as a ceramic pitcher, but better than nothing.

Margot disengaged the dead bolt on the door, hands trembling as she looked for Letitia. She'd open the door then grab a shovel and go back to get Rett.

As she turned the knob, she heard a muffled cry. Her gaze swung toward the fire pit, surprised that the woman had managed to get around her. But it wasn't Letitia. In the shadows, trussed like a holiday turkey, Hiram Potter stared at her with wild eyes. A gag covered his soot-smeared, sweaty face.

"Hiram!" Margot abandoned the door and hurried to him. She pulled the gag out of his mouth. "Are you hurt?"

A thousand questions ran through her head, but they'd have time for those later. She hoped.

Hiram winced. "My head. What are you doing here, Margot? She's going to kill us."

"You need to go. Now." She grabbed his arm and tried to help him to his feet. "I have to find Rett."

"Too late."

Margot swung around to face the source of the voice, her grip tight on Hiram's arm.

Letitia Jacobs stood two dozen feet away, revolver pointed at them. "I shot her," she said.

A whimper escaped Margot's throat. Her lifelong directive, *Don't let them see you flinch,* evaporated. "You horrible bitch," she snarled.

"I warned you. You could have paid the fifty thousand and ended this, but no." Letitia raised the gun, gripping it in both hands to steady her aim. "A good businesswoman knows when to cut her losses, Miss Harriman."

Margot caught movement from behind Letitia. Something swung toward the woman's left side. Margot dragged Hiram to the ground as the gun went off with a loud bang. Letitia stumbled sideways. The weapon flew from her hand. She fell against a table of scrap bits, then slid to the ground with a crash of metal.

Rett stood behind her, holding a long-handled shovel poised to strike again. She was filthy and disheveled, a red stain spreading across her side. "Stickball skills came in handy. That would've been a home run."

"Rett!" Relief made Margot light-headed. Leaving Hiram on the ground, she rushed to Rett, hugging her awkwardly around her improvised weapon. Rett grunted, and Margot released her. "You're hurt."

"A scratch." Rett dropped the shovel with a clang. She moved the panel of her coat aside and touched the torn and stained bodice of her blouse. She hissed in pain. "Maybe more than a scratch." Meeting Margot's gaze, she asked, "Are you all right?"

Margot could only nod, the enormity of the last few minutes—what could have been the last few minutes of her life—starting to sink in. Her teeth chattered. She tightened her jaws and swallowed. Now was not the time. "Yes, but Hiram is hurt. We need to get him to the hospital, and get you looked at as well."

Rett glanced at Hiram, then at the unconscious Letitia. "Calling for help means letting the police know what's happened. Are you sure you want to do that?"

Margot had wanted to keep everything and anything about B&H possibly being involved in something terrible out of the public eye. The idea of the papers getting the chance to twist and turn around facts made her sick. But Letitia Martin Jacobs had tried to kill them. Hiram and Rett were injured. Other people had been hurt or worse. It was time to face the truth and begin the process of reparations.

"I am," she said. "Stay here with Hiram and Letitia. I'll go call for the police and an ambulance. Then I'll call my lawyers."

Thirty-Four

Rett eased back against the cushion of one of the half dozen wicker lawn chairs arranged in a semicircle on Margot Harriman's back patio. The plaster on her side pulled at the healing skin, making her wince. She'd been lucky, both that Letitia hadn't hit something vital and that she hadn't come over to make sure Rett was dead after shooting her in the shadows of the metal racks. Dropping as if fatally wounded had given Rett the chance to sneak up on the murderous woman while she went for Margot.

She shivered at the memory of the look of fear on Margot's face. Yes, they had been very lucky.

Out on the neatly clipped lawn, CeeCee and Shiloh were dominating Danny and Sid in a rousing game of croquet.

"You cheated!" Danny yelled to his sister. "You moved my ball."

Shiloh gave him her signature cocky grin. "Prove it."

"I don't have to prove it. I grew up with you."

CeeCee and Sid laughed. Rett smiled. The Wallaces were never boring, that was for sure. She was glad Margot had invited them along for this casual little gathering. It was a perfect bluebird-sky day, and they all deserved a bit of fun.

"Who's winning?" Margot asked as she handed Rett a Bloody Mary. She sat in a neighboring chair with her own tall glass.

Rett moved the celery stalk aside and sipped her drink. The tang of the tomato juice and the kick of the vodka were perfectly balanced. "CeeCee and Shiloh, though both sides are cheating mercilessly. Actually, only Shiloh and Danny are cheating. CeeCee and Sid are taking turns being alternately outraged and supportive, depending on if it benefits their team."

Margot laughed, drawing Shiloh's attention. Grinning, she raised her glass to the blonde. Shiloh winked at Margot, then went back to annoying her brother.

Rett was glad to see Margot genuinely relaxed and happy. In the two weeks since Letitia Martin Jacobs held them at the point of a gun, Margot had been derided by the press and public. Word had gotten out once Letitia was in custody and questioned. The Yonkers police and ambulance crew had heard an earful from the woman, who accused Margot and Rett of trespassing (true) and assault (also true, but justified). Despite implicating herself, Letitia didn't hold back.

Even before the story of the contaminated cans and medical fraud broke to the public, Margot couldn't get into a defensive position fast enough. And once it was in the papers, everything she had hoped to avoid had hit her square in the face. Though her lawyers were at the ready, the news caused an uproar and financial backlash as people called for charges to be filed and B&H to be shut down.

The statement Margot had put out through her lawyers didn't admit guilt, though it acknowledged there were concerns about B&H using Martin Scrap & Metal Fabrication materials. Laboratory tests on metal samples from Martin's and from the B&H cannery had confirmed everyone's fears: there were significantly higher levels of lead and arsenic in the samples than considered safe.

Margot had immediately issued a recall, noting those potentially dangerous cans had a particular mark. Any product in stores or homes could be returned and replaced, free of charge. She also organized an investigation into those who had sickened or died in the last few years. Several families had been compensated with the potential for more to come.

Rett had wondered how much it was costing B&H. Margot told her it didn't matter.

"I can't ignore people falling ill, or worse," she'd said. "It's not just a matter of my reputation. It's the right thing to do."

The papers had had a field day, of course. Most applauded her after their initial outrage. Some continued to call for B&H to be criminally charged. When two or three food safety advocates spoke up in Margot's defense for her efforts after the fact, the public slowly started to come around. Though for B&H, the proof would be in forthcoming sales reports.

Even the B&H shareholders had supported her, praising her quick response to the Martin fraud and endangerment to the public as having saved lives. One gentleman had been quoted in an article, saying her leadership was an asset to the company. Margot had confided to Rett that the particular individual had stood up for her at the latest shareholders' emergency meeting, stating she had "performed as well as any man would have." High compliments indeed, considering the source and the audience. She was the right person—man or woman—to helm B&H through any boon or crisis, and they knew it as well as Margot did.

The State of New York, however, had their own take on the situation. There had been whispers and not quite whispers of criminal charges. B&H lawyers managed to get those tossed and the state settled for fines and probation. Their Division of Food Safety and Inspection would be increasing the frequency of their visits, both planned and surprise. Margot welcomed the decision, even if her accountants whimpered at the size of the checks they were writing.

The lady herself had shown little stress, at least in public. Concern, yes, and heartfelt regrets about the situation, yet always in control. But Rett knew that beneath that calm exterior the enormity of what could still come to pass ate at Margot. Rett hadn't been with her every minute, having to deal with her own falling-out with Albert, but the times they got together she saw the bruise-like shadows under Margot's eyes, her appetite nearly nonexistent, her drinks getting larger and more frequent. Margot was cooperating with the authorities, but there was real concern for people who had been or could still be hurt by tainted cans, and that she could lose everything.

Letitia Jacobs was in jail, awaiting trial for intentional harm, violations of the 1906 Pure Food and Drug Act, the assault of Hiram Potter and Rett herself, conspiracy to commit murder, attempted murder, and falsifying state records. Her delivery driver—who also turned out to be her lover, much to her husband Calvin's surprise—had been charged with the murder of Charles Meade. Letitia had named him in an attempt to ease the heat on herself, but then he turned around and gave a statement against her not just for the murder plot, but for the fraud and switching of materials going on at Martin Scrap & Metal Fabrication. He'd likely be convicted, but his cooperation might spare him the electric chair. Letitia would be going nowhere for a long, long time.

Rett felt sorry for Calvin, the poor sap. He'd known nothing and had as much of an uphill battle to regain public trust as Margot did. Maybe more so, since he didn't have lawyers to buffer the blows.

The papers mostly focused on the connection between Martin's and B&H. There was little mention of the medical fraud cases, which again, Margot had her lawyers and accountants deal with. No hospitals, insurance companies, or real people had been harmed, so that was a little easier to clear up with reimbursements and penalties. The cash in the J. Ferrier safety-deposit box had come in handy for that.

Hiram Potter's role in the fraud and the contaminated metal scheme was still a little shaky to Rett. Giana Gilroy had gone to him months before and confessed the entire thing. She'd shown him the old hospital receipt book she'd used to falsify visits, accidentally packed by her late husband when he'd left his job as a hospital accounting clerk to take a position at the J. Ferrier Bank and Trust. Mrs. Gilroy had come across the book, but never got around to disposing of it. When she needed to come up with a plan to get money for Meade, the receipt book came to mind.

Hiram had told her to destroy the book, said he'd handle it, and she was not to tell Margot. But he hadn't handled it. He'd been willing to continue letting Letitia provide substandard materials and paying off Meade until he could figure out a plan, which he hadn't. Mrs. Gilroy couldn't bear the deceit

A MURDEROUS BUSINESS

and lies to Margot. Unfortunately, she'd died in the middle of her confession, and Potter was still at a loss. Confronting Letitia got him bashed on the head, tied up, and slated for a visit to the Martin smelter. He was damn lucky Rett and Margot had gone to Yonkers that day.

Things were settling down, the papers and the public on to the next headline grabber, though Rett was sure they were keeping an eye on Margot and B&H.

For now, however, Margot was able to take a breath.

"Have you heard from Hiram?" Rett asked.

Margot replied without taking her attention from the croquet game. "He's recovering and enjoying retirement with his family in Philadelphia. Which reminds me, I need to find a new manager."

"Mr. Thorpe would do well." Though she hadn't spent much time with the B&H foreman, his rapport with the workers would be an advantage.

Margot nodded. "He would at that."

CeeCee swung her mallet, her yellow ball flying across the lawn, through the wicket, and against the post beside Shiloh's red ball. She and Shiloh threw up their hands and whooped in celebration. Danny glared at his sister, calling for a another match, while Sid smiled and shrugged.

"I don't mean to drag business up on such a lovely day," Margot said, glancing in Rett's direction, "but how are things with you and Albert?"

Rett took a generous sip of her drink, giving herself time to respond. She had told Margot about the way Albert had reacted to her and CeeCee being a couple, about him throwing her out of the office. Eventually, Mama had managed to settle him, saying it wasn't up to them to determine who their children fell in love with. She'd also convinced him that it was time to go into full retirement and travel as they'd always planned. That left Mancini & Associates without the foundation of a reputable investigator.

"Still working it out," she finally said. "I have a few small cases to finish up, then I don't know."

She shrugged, unable to finish the thought because she had no idea what she was going to do next. Most of the capital belonged to her parents. They'd need what was there to live, let alone any travel. Rett could keep things afloat with the sorts of cases she was currently taking, but only for so long.

"Maybe find a regular job and take cases on the side."

"I have a proposition for you," Margot said.

"You know I'm with CeeCee." Rett grinned at Margot's mock stunned expression.

"Very funny. A business proposition. I'll cover overhead costs for the next, oh, five years, while you work cases to build your reputation and client list."

Rett's joking mood evaporated like water on a hot pan. "You want to finance my business? I can't have you do that. Not just because it feels strange taking money from you."

"First of all, I'd consider it a loan which you'd have for five years before starting to pay it back if you needed. We can work out terms and a schedule that satisfies us both. Second, by the look of terror on your face, you're concerned I'd want to have a say in every little thing. Again, not the case. We can put that in writing as well." Margot's smile was reassuring. "I don't want to be your investigation partner, Rett. I want you to have the chance to do what you love. I consider it an investment."

It sounded too good to be true, which meant one thing in Rett's experience. "No strings?"

Margot pressed her lips together. "Well, one string."

Ah, there it was.

"If I need your services," she continued, "I don't get charged your going rate, only expenses."

On the surface, Rett could see the advantages of having the financial boost. Who wouldn't jump at it? But to be beholden to someone? A bank wouldn't have say in how she ran her agency.

Yeah, but what bank is going to give you a business loan?

A valid question.

"You'd have to stay out of the cases I take and the nonfinancial decisions I make. Are you willing to do that, Margot?" It had been difficult keeping the woman from involvement in her own case, of course, but that was different. She hoped.

"I think I can manage. I'll get paperwork started Monday morning, if you're amenable."

"I think I am." Rett held her half-full glass out. "To a silent, hands-off, financial partnership, Miss Harriman."

Margot grinned and gently clinked her glass against Rett's. "To a prosperous partnership and our continued friendship, Miss Mancini."

Acknowledgments

This is my ninth novel-length book. You'd think that by now I'd have certain aspects down. But every book is different. Every team you work with is different. Every situation and moment in your life is different. Even things that are mostly the same are different. There is a balance of familiar and new, the comfort of knowing what's to come and the thrill of another adventure in the process. I have been incredibly lucky with those whom I have shared these experiences, and I'm grateful for them all.

Lovely Agent™ Natalie Lakosil has been looking out for me and kicking me in the arse (gently) since before I was published. She has always been upfront and real. Thank you for

ACKNOWLEDGMENTS

your patience and expertise, Natalie. I'd be a messier hot mess without you.

The team at Minotaur continually impresses me with their skills, knowledge, talent, and enthusiasm. From the get-go, editor Vanessa Aguirre was gung-ho about Margot, Rett, and the gang. She offered keen insights into the story, asked the right questions, and let me tell the tale I wanted to tell. Thank you for seeing *A Murderous Business* for what it was and what it could be, Vanessa. The publicity and marketing folks, Ana Couto, Paul Hochman, Kayla Janas, and Juchole Gains, put together a campaign to be proud of. I'm grateful for their energy, ideas, and support.

I can't say enough about the rest of the Minotaur team: publishing director Kelley Ragland, editorial director Catherine Richards, designer Omar Chapa and jacket designer David Rotstein (this book has one of the most beautiful covers ever!), mechanical designer Rowen Davis, managing editor Alisa Trager, production editor John Morrone, and production manager Catharine Turiano. And to Sabrina Roberts, the copyeditor who sussed out details I missed or messed up: Blessings on you! All mistakes are mine. We may never have communicated directly, but you have all been so very important in making the production of *A Murderous Business* smooth and joyful. Thank you!

Many, many thanks to my loving family and friends who

ACKNOWLEDGMENTS

put up with constant "Did you know . . ." and "So the idea is . . ." conversations. You have seen me through more plot knots and character developments than you realize.

Finally, a huge thank you to all you readers. I'm glad we found each other.

About the Author

Cathy Pegau started her writing journey with sword-and-sorcery fantasy and science-fiction romance, but also loves the challenge of trying new things. While researching local history for an Alaska-based postapocalyptic pirate tale, she learned of some real-life events that spurred the creation of the Charlotte Brody Mysteries, a historical mystery series set in her current town. These events also piqued her latent interest in history in general. Though her recent works have been historicals, both with and without paranormal elements, she writes what catches her fancy. Anything is possible, as long as there's a good story and interesting characters. Cathy lives in a small fishing town in Alaska with her spouse, pets, and the occasional black bear wandering through the yard.